DAMAGE

DAMAGE

a novel by
JOSEPHINE HART

ALFRED A. KNOPF
NEW YORK
1991

Library of Congress Cataloging-in-Publication Data
Hart, Josephine.
   Damage : a novel / by Josephine Hart. — 1st ed.
   p.   cm.
   ISBN 0-679-40135-0
   I. Title.
PR6058.A694845D36   1991
813'.54—dc20   90-53393
                                                   CIP

Manufactured in the United States of America
First American Edition

To Maurice Saatchi

DAMAGE

ONE

There is an internal landscape, a geography of the soul; we search for its outlines all our lives.

Those who are lucky enough to find it ease like water over a stone, onto its fluid contours, and are home.

Some find it in the place of their birth; others may leave a seaside town, parched, and find themselves refreshed in the desert. There are those born in rolling countryside who are really only at ease in the intense and busy loneliness of the city.

For some, the search is for the imprint of another; a child or a mother, a grandfather or a brother, a lover, a husband, a wife, or a foe.

We may go through our lives happy or unhappy, successful or unfulfilled, loved or unloved, without ever standing cold with the shock of recognition, without ever feeling the agony as the twisted iron in our soul unlocks itself and we slip at last into place.

I have been at the bedsides of the dying, who looked puzzled at their family's grief as they left a world in which they had never felt at home.

I have seen men weep more at the death of their brother, whose being had once locked into theirs, than at the death of their child. I have watched brides become mothers, who only once, long ago, were radiant on their uncle's knee.

And in my own life, I have travelled far, acquiring loved and unfamiliar companions; a wife, a son, and a daughter. I have lived with them, a loving alien in surroundings of unsatisfying beauty. An efficient dissembler, I gently and silently smoothed the rough edges of my being. I hid the awkwardness and pain with which I inclined towards my chosen outline, and tried to be what those I loved expected me to be—a good husband, a good father, and a good son.

Had I died at fifty I would have been a doctor, and an established politician, though not a household name. One who had made a contribution, and was much loved by his sorrowing wife, Ingrid, and by his children, Martyn and Sally.

My funeral would have been well attended by those who had gone further in life than I, and who therefore honoured my memory by their presence. And by those who believed they had loved the private man, and by their tears gave testimony to his existence.

It would have been the funeral of an above-average man, more generously endowed with the world's blessings than most. A man who, at the comparatively early age of fifty, had ended his journey. A journey which would certainly have led to some greater honour and achievement, had it continued.

But I did not die in my fiftieth year. There are few who know me now, who do not regard that as a tragedy.

TWO

They say that childhood forms us, that those early influences are the key to everything. Is the peace of the soul so easily won? Simply the inevitable result of a happy childhood. What makes childhood happy? Parental harmony? Good health? Security? Might not a happy childhood be the worst possible preparation for life? Like leading a lamb to the slaughter.

My childhood, adolescence, and young manhood were dominated by my father.

Will, the total power of will, was his fundamental credo.

'Will. Man's greatest asset. Underused by the majority. The solution to all life's problems.' How often had I heard those words.

The combination of his unquestioning belief in his own power to dictate his life, and the tall, heavy body in which this will resided, made him a most formidable man.

His name was Tom. To this day, years after his death, I associate strength of character with every Tom I meet.

From the small grocery business his father left him, he built a chain of retail shops that made him a wealthy man. But he would have been successful at whatever career he pursued. He would have applied his will to the pursuit of his goal, and inevitably have achieved it.

He applied his will to his business, to his wife, and to his son. His first goal with my mother had been to win her. Then, to ensure that any way of life she pursued did not interfere with the other goals of his life.

He wooed her with total dedication, and married her within six months of meeting her. The nature of the attraction between them is still a mystery to me. My mother does not seem to me to have been a beauty. I heard her once described as having been a vivacious young woman. Perhaps that was what had attracted him. However, there is no trace of vivacity in my recollection of her gentle presence. She painted as a young girl. Some of her watercolours decorated the walls of my childhood home. But she stopped. Suddenly. I have never learned why. The nature of the bond between them, for it was undoubtedly there, still eludes me.

I was an only child. After my birth they slept in separate rooms. Perhaps my birth had caused trauma. Whatever the reason, there was my father's room, and my mother's room, and they were separate. How did that young man live his sexual life? I have heard no scandalous stories, overheard no innuendos. Perhaps the purpose of separate rooms was not to banish sexual activity, but to curtail it, for reasons of contraception.

My life as a child, and as a young boy, seems shrouded in a mist, permeated by the constant power of my father's presence. 'Make up your mind about it. Then do it,' my father would say—about exams, running (my only athletic prowess), even the piano lessons which I took, much to his embarrassment. 'Make up your mind. Then do it.'

But what of uncertainty, or pleasant failure? What of the will of others, subjected to his own? Perhaps it was something he never thought about. Not through callousness or cruelty, but because he truly believed he knew best. And that everyone's best interest would be served by following his.

THREE

"So you have made up your mind to be a doctor?" my father said, when at eighteen I decided to study medicine.

"Yes."

"Good! Stick with it. It's a tough course. Can you stick with it?"

"Yes."

"I never wanted you to come in with me. I have always said, 'Just make up your own mind what you want to do. Then do it.'"

"Yes."

Even as I went my own way, I felt I served some purpose of his. So it is with powerful personalities. As we swim and dive away from them, we still feel the water is theirs.

"Why that's wonderful," my mother said. "You're sure it's what you want?"

"Yes."

Neither of them asked me why. If they had, I could not have answered. It was a vague feeling that just grew. If it had been thwarted, perhaps I would have found clear-cut reasons, and been passionate in my commitment. Perhaps that sort of passion only comes when the will is thwarted.

At eighteen I went to Cambridge and started my medical studies. Though I studied the myriad ills of the body and ways to soothe them, this brought me no closer to my fellow man. I seemed not to care about him or love him, any more than if I had studied economics. There was something missing in me, and in my commitment. Still, I qualified, and decided to become a GP.

"Why not specialise?" my father said. "Become a Consultant."

"No."

"Can't see you as a GP."

"Oh?"

"Ah, well! I see you have made up your mind."

I joined a practice in St. John's Wood. I bought a flat. My life began to take shape. Free will had brought me there, not parental pressure, not terrible academic struggle. I had made up my mind. I had done it.

The next step was obvious.

"Ingrid is a living beauty," my father said. "Strength of character, too! There is great will power in that girl," he continued approvingly. "Made up your mind to marry then?"

"Yes."

"Good. Good. Marriage is good . . ." He paused. ". . . for the soul."

All my ambitions were fulfilled. All had been my own choice. It was a blessed life. It was a good life. But whose life?

FOUR

My wife is beautiful. For that, I have the evidence of my own eyes, and the reaction of those who meet her.

Hers is a beauty of pleasing proportions, a felicitous blending of eyes, skin, and hair. She is complete. She was complete before I met her. It was to her picture of life that I contributed my being. And I was happy to do so.

She was twenty when I met her, conventionally, correctly at a friend's house. There was nothing about her that jarred or caused me pain. She possessed in great measure the powerful seductiveness of serenity. Ingrid took my initial admiration, and later love, as a treasured gift, but a deserved one.

I, who had feared love, feared some wildness it might unleash in me, was soothed. I was allowed to love. I believed myself loved in return.

I unfolded no mysteries with her. She was in all ways as I had imagined she would be. Her body was warm, and beautiful. If she never approached me, neither did she ever turn away.

Marriage is not the gamble we sometimes say it is. Over its course we have some control. Our choice of spouse is mostly intelligent, as well as romantic. For who is foolhardy in an endeavour whose reputation is so fearful? My marriage to Ingrid pursued a course which surprised neither of us. As loving as we could have expected, as careful as our natures seemed to demand.

No. Children are the great gamble. From the moment they are born, our helplessness increases. Instead of being ours to mould and shape after our best knowledge and endeavour, they are themselves. From their birth they are the centre of our lives, and the dangerous edge of existence.

Their health, a random good fortune at best, is often regarded by us as the result of breeding and care. Their illnesses, when serious, destroy happiness. When they recover, we live for years with the knowledge of what their death could mean to us. The arbitrary nature of our passion for children, who reveal so little of themselves during their short stay with us, is, for many, life's great romance. But, unlike the object of our romantic love, we do not choose the child who will be our son or daughter.

No earthshaking revelations on the nature of life seemed to attend Martyn's entry into the world. He was there, almost as though we had always expected him, a loved and perfect son. Sally was born two years later. My family was complete.

In my thirties I looked at my small children gratefully, lovingly, and lost. Surely here was the centre of life, its core? A woman, two children, a home. I was on high ground. I was safe.

We had the serenity and happiness of those who have never known unhappiness or terrible anxiety. The much admired peace of our home was a good fortune for which we secretly congratulated ourselves, as though some high moral purpose of ours had been served. Perhaps we had learned that life was open to organisation to one's own advantage; that it simply required intelligence and determination; a system, a formula, a trick.

Perhaps there are benign and malevolent rhythms in life. We had tuned ours to the sound of beauty. My life then was like a pleasant landscape. The trees were green, the lawns rich, the lake calm.

Sometimes, I gazed at my wife asleep, and knew that if I wakened her I would have nothing to say. What could they be, the questions I wanted her to answer? My answers were all there, down the hallway, in Martyn's room or Sally's. How could I have questions still? What right had I to questions?

Time rode through my life—a victor. I barely even clung to the reins.

When we mourn those who die young—those who have been robbed of time—we weep for lost joys. We weep for opportunities and pleasures we ourselves have never known. We feel sure that somehow that young body would have known the yearning delight for which we searched in vain all our lives. We believe that the untried soul, trapped inside its young prison, might have flown free and known the joy that we still seek.

We say that life is sweet, its satisfactions deep. All this we say, as we sleepwalk our time through years of days and nights. We let time cascade over us like a waterfall, believing it to be never ending. Yet each day that touches us, and every man in the world, is unique; irredeemable; over. And just another Monday.

Ah, but those lost Mondays of our young dead friend!

How much better they would have been! Years pass. Decades pass. And living has not been done.

But what of the births I had attended? Could anything mark a man's time more usefully? What of the deaths I had witnessed? A competent easer of pain, I was often the last person the dying saw. Were my eyes kind? Did I show fear? I believe I was useful, here. What of all the minor dramas? The fears and anguish I dealt with? Here, surely, was time well spent.

Yet to what end did time cascade then, only to be lost in the flood? Why was I a doctor? Why did I minister? To what good purpose did I minister, carefully but without love?

Those who are lucky should hide. They should be grateful. They should hope the days of wrath will not visit their home. They should run to protect all that is theirs, and pity their neighbour when the horror strikes. But quietly, and from a distance.

FIVE

Ingrid's father was a Conservative MP. He had been born into a well-off middle-class family and was now, through wise investment, a wealthy man. Though my father had more money than most people would have believed, Edward Thompson was the wealthier man.

He believed that the basic instinct of mankind is greed. That the party which won an election was the one which promised the most advantageous economic package to the majority, not to the country.

"That's where Labour makes its big mistake, old boy. They know it's all about economics really. They confuse that with a better economic deal for everyone. No one wants it. It's too expensive, and anyway they just don't care. The majority, keep them better off, and they will vote for you. It's as simple as that."

Ingrid smiled, or argued gently, humorously. But the reality was, he could be right. He was returned each election, his safe majority still intact.

I found it harder to be gentle with him, but all my questions went unasked for many years. As time went on, I became less patient. I began to argue with him more and more forcefully. To my astonishment, he loved it. He rose to every criticism, his face beaming with delight. He was a far more skilled debater than I had ever imagined. He roared with triumphant laughter whenever he had me cornered.

My position was inherently a weak one, I suppose. I loathed Socialism, and what seemed to me the simplistic solutions of the Left. I hated the lack of freedom for which the Left increasingly stood.

I accepted the basic philosophy of the Conservative Party. However, its total dedication to the pursuit of personal material wealth, I found deeply unattractive. I was a questioning, challenging, dissatisfied Conservative. But I was still a Conservative at heart.

Medicine is not the best training for the political mind. This was painfully obvious in many of the debates, though with practise, I improved.

"Why don't you stand for Parliament? There's room in the Party for a chap like you."

My father-in-law could have been issuing an invitation to dinner at his club, so casually did he drop this bombshell into the conversation one evening.

"Yes, yes! You are a doctor. You stand for compassion, integrity, for keeping us greedier chaps on the straight and narrow. I like the idea. It's good for the Party. It's good for you. You could go far, you know. Oh, yes. Didn't think so at first, of course. You seemed a bit bloody inarticulate, if you don't mind my saying so. But you've come along a treat. It's all there, always was, under the surface you know. I have seen it before, quiet chap suddenly blossoms. Then you have the great talkers in their twenties, who in their forties have nothing to say. Oh, yes. I've seen it all. Twenty-eight years I've been an MP, twenty-eight years. I've seen it all."

Ingrid smiled, conspiratorially I thought afterwards.

But I was flattered. I arrogantly believed that I could soften Edward Thompson's brand of Conservatism, just a little, and make my own contribution. My inner doubts slipped away that night. I was pleased with the idea. I was proud of myself.

After years of carefully watching every move I made in order to avoid being dominated by my own father, I now found myself about to embark on a whole new course in life, because my father-in-law had flattered me into it.

Ingrid and I sat and talked more intensely that evening than at any time in our marriage. She was very excited. I realised that she must always have hero-worshiped her father. She was now thrilled by the thought of my following in his footsteps.

We agreed I would pursue a safe seat, which had just become vacant close to where we lived. There my influence as a doctor would be at its most powerful. Though I was opposed by a clever, older, local businessman, Party officials clearly wanted a member of the "caring" professions. I was quickly selected as a Tory candidate. At the by-election they must have felt they had made the right decision, because I was elected with a substantially increased majority. Ingrid retired into herself again, satisfied. The normal working mechanism of our relationship reestablished itself. She was content. The tranquillity which had always characterised our daily lives returned.

Years later, I often wondered how much had been discussed between Ingrid and her father, before the fateful dinner party. Had they found me so easy to manipulate? Or was my guard so low with them, as with everyone, because I thought myself unknown by anyone, and unthreatened?

I was an adman's dream. I was forty-five, with a beautiful and intelligent wife, a son at Oxford, and a daughter at public school. My father had been a well-known businessman. My father-in-law was a leading politician who had paid his dues to the Party.

I was reasonably good looking. Not handsome enough for my supposed good looks to precede me, like some ill-deserved reputation, but enough to be pleasing on television—the new gladiatorial arena. There, those who combat to the political death salute not Caesar, but the people whom they are about to betray. This gives the masses an illusion of power which serves to hide the fact that, however bloody the battle to the death seems, the politician always wins. In a democracy, some politician, somewhere, is always winning.

I intended to be the politician who won. My suit was a strong one. I was elected and rose to higher ranks with the ease that had attended all my endeavours. I believed as strongly in my cause as I did in medicine. But neither endeavour had cost me anything. Time, for a man who has never truly felt a second of it, is not a great sacrifice; nor is effort that brings worthwhile results; nor energy from a man in middle years and perfect health.

In politics I committed myself to the same old values I had practised in a busy surgery—honesty, a kind of prickly integrity, a total lack of interest in personal power, combined with the maddening arrogance of one who knows that, if he decided to play, he would win.

I avoided all the basic suppositions on which parliamentary life is based. Loyalty to the Party as a form of self-advancement, the trading off of favours, the recognition and grudging acceptance of emerging leaders—the masters of the future, who need to be acknowledged and have fealty sworn to them—all this I found repugnant.

However, to appear unambitious amongst the ambitious is to invite loathing or fear. To be in the game, but not playing with intent to win, is to be the enemy.

It was improbable, but not impossible, for me to emerge at the top. All I needed was the cutting edge. Perhaps I did not have it. Or perhaps it was just hidden. I became an enigma to my colleagues—a seemingly purposeful man, but without a purpose. My obvious abilities were as yet untested, but my colleagues and I were aware that should the chance come, success would probably follow. But why should the chance be given to me? Unlike so many others, I did not lust for it.

I had not found the key to myself in any area of service, medical or political. I carried out my constituency surgeries with the same absolute involvement with which I had attended my patients. But it was the absolute of the intellect. No effort seemed too great to advise on this matter, or act on another.

My thoroughness and expertise bred a respect, and a kind of confidence. I was doing the job well. There was no doubt about that. I spoke out on subjects which seemed to me to need comment. I said what I meant. I meant what I said. The political consequences were not weighed by me, at least not unduly. On the other hand, the subjects on which I spoke out strongly were hardly fundamental to Party discipline. My ideas were attractive to large numbers of the Tory Left.

I never faced a serious moral dilemma. Nothing that I felt or said was extreme, or left me completely out on a limb. All options, except those of the far Right, were open to me still. Had I planned the perfect political life for myself, it could not have worked better.

I was soon given the post of junior minister in the Department of Health, to which I was obviously suited. My concerned face and well-bred voice spouting acceptable, vaguely liberal clichés appeared on television. Or I gazed earnestly from newspapers and magazines, saying the things I'd always believed, in what came across as a sincere and genuine manner. I learned the public geography of my soul from television and newspapers. It was neither shaming nor pleasing, just another perfect set piece. Even I recognised that if I kept up this performance for some time, I might shine even more brightly as the years went by.

One poll, published in a Sunday paper, listed me amongst the possible future Prime Ministers. Ingrid was thrilled. My children were embarrassed.

I acted those parts required of me, like some professional member of a good English repertory company. Reliable, competent, taking pride in my work, but as far away from the magic of an Olivier or a Gielgud as not to seem part of the profession at all.

The passion that transforms life, and art, did not seem to be mine. But in all its essentials, my life was a good performance.

SIX

My son was a handsome young man. If there was in me a slight stockiness, Ingrid's slender proportions tempered it in Martyn. He had both height and strength. Ingrid's excessive paleness was there. My dark hair and eyes seemed to counterpoint the almost feminine delicacy of his skin. His was a dramatic colouring, unusual in England, and the exact opposite of his sister Sally's. She was that rare yet common miracle, the true English rose.

Beauty in our children is disturbing. There is an implied excess that casts a question mark over the parents. Most fathers would like their daughters to be attractive, their sons to be manly. But true beauty disconcerts. Like genius we wish it on another family.

Martyn's looks and elegance embarrassed me. His sexual involvements were so blatantly casual, that it astounded me his girlfriends saw no danger in him. The succession of young women, whom Ingrid and I met at Sunday lunches or at occasional parties, seemed never ending. I realised that my son was sexually promiscuous. He was undoubtedly careless of the many loving looks sent in his direction. Ingrid was amused by it all. I was much less so.

His attitude to life, when he left university, dismayed

me. Medicine was of no interest. Politics was unappeal-
ing to him. He wanted to be a journalist—the onlooker's
position in life, it seemed to me. He was very ambitious
and determined about his career, but his ambition was totally for himself. At no time did he delude himself, or us.

He got a job on a local paper, where amusingly and
perhaps to his chagrin, he was made political correspon-
dent. When he was twenty-three, he got a junior journalist's job on a Fleet Street newspaper. He left the small
flat we had created for him over the garage, and found
a place of his own.

Ingrid was pleased by his success, and single-minded-
ness. It was such a flattering contrast to the sons of our
friends, who seemed so unsure of everything. To me,
however, he remained an enigma. I looked at him sometimes and reminded myself that he was my son. He would
shoot a questioning look back at me, and smile. I knew
that with Martyn my performance was only adequate.

With Sally, I fared a little better. She was earnest and
sweet. Her small talent for painting she developed to its
highest potential. She became a junior in the design department of a publishing company.

So here was a marriage, its outlines clear. I was a faithful, if not passionate husband, and I acted lovingly and
responsibly towards my children. I had seen them safely
through to young adulthood. My ambitions, in important and respected fields, had been realised. I had enough
money from income, and private means, to put me beyond financial worry.

What man was luckier?

I had obeyed the rules. I had been rewarded.

Clear direction, some luck, and here I was, fifty and
fully realised.

SEVEN

I have sometimes looked at old photographs of the smiling faces of victims, and searched them desperately for some sign that they knew. Surely they must have known that within hours or days their life was to end in that car crash, in that aeroplane disaster, or in domestic tragedy. But I can find no sign whatever. Nothing. They look out serenely, a terrible warning to us all. 'No I didn't know. Just like you . . . there were no signs.' 'I who died at thirty . . . I too had planned my forties.' 'I who died at twenty had dreamed, as you do, of the roses round the cottage someday. It could happen to you. Why not? Why me? Why you? Why not?'

So I know that in whatever photographs were taken of me at that time, my face will gaze back at you confident, a trifle cold, but basically unknowing. It is the face of a man I no longer understand. I know the bridge that connects me to him. But the other side has disappeared. Disappeared like some piece of land the sea has overtaken. There may be some landmarks on the beach, at low tide, but that is all.

"She looks older than you. Not a lot. But how old is she?"

"She's thirty-three."

"Well, that's eight years older than you, Martyn."

"So what?"

"So nothing. Just the fact that she is eight years older than you."

"Who are you talking about?" I asked. We were in the kitchen.

"Anna Barton, Martyn's latest girlfriend."

"Oh. She's new isn't she?"

"Oh, God. You make me sound as if I'm some sort of Casanova."

"Well, aren't you?"

"No." Martyn sounded sad. "Or if I was once, it's finished. Well, anyway, I just never met anyone who mattered."

"Does she?"

"Who?"

"This Anna Burton."

"Barton. Anna Barton. I've only known her for a few months. Well, she's more important than the others."

"Brighter too," said Sally.

"Oh, you'd recognise a bright girl would you, Sally? She'd be something like you no doubt."

"There are many different types of intelligence, Martyn. Mine's artistic. Yours is for words. That's all. But you couldn't draw a cat to save your life."

The Sally who had blushed or cried at Martyn's attacks was long gone. She was not close to her brother, and depended on him not at all. The subject of Anna Barton was dropped quietly with the Sunday post-lunch conversation. She was not referred to again by either Martyn or Sally.

"You don't like this Anna person then?" I asked Ingrid as we prepared for bed.

She paused for a long time and then said:

"No. No, I don't."

"Why? Surely it's not just because she's eight years older than Martyn."

"Partly. No, she makes me uneasy."

"Oh, well it's probably nothing. Knowing Martyn, it's just another of his flirtations," I said.

"No, it's more, I feel sure."

"Oh? How did I miss out on meeting her?"

"She came here a few times last month when you were in Cambridge. Then another time for supper when you were in Edinburgh."

"Pretty?"

"Strange looking. Not really pretty. Looks her age I thought. Not many girls do nowadays."

"You certainly don't," I said to Ingrid. I was bored now with the subject of Anna Barton and I could tell that it distressed Ingrid.

"Thank you." She smiled at me.

And Ingrid certainly did not look close to fifty. The same slim blonde beauty remained, slightly less smooth. The eyes were less bright but she was a beautiful woman, undoubtedly. A woman who would remain beautiful for a very long time to come. She still seemed as impregnable as ever. Blonde, cool, beautiful. My wife, Ingrid, Edward's daughter, Martyn and Sally's mother.

Her life and mine had run on parallel lines during all these years. No crashes, no unread signals. We were a civilised couple, approaching our later years with equanimity.

EIGHT

"Anna Barton, meet Roger Hughes."

"How do you do?"

The introduction going on behind me seemed as though it were happening in a silent room. In fact I was at the packed Christmas party of a newspaper publisher. In his wife's Mayfair gallery each year he gathered his world around him in a seductive, dangerous bear hug. Then everyone was released into a free fall for the rest of the year, as though all the tribulations his paper would cause his guests before the following Christmas were already forgiven.

Why didn't I look round? Why, out of normal curiosity, or politeness, or concern, did I not approach this girl? Why did "How do you do?" sound significant? Its formality seemed deliberate. Her voice was very deep, clear, and unfriendly.

"Anna, I want you to see this."

"Hello, Dominick."

Another voice claimed her and she seemed, silently, to move away. I felt uneasy. I felt out of tune with everything. I was preparing to make my goodbyes, when suddenly she stood in front of me and said:

"You are Martyn's father. I'm Anna Barton, and I felt I ought to introduce myself."

The woman who stood before me was tall, pale, with short black wavy hair swept off her face. She was a figure in a black suit and smiled not at all.

"Hello, I'm so glad to meet you. I seem to have missed you each time you've been to the house."

"I've only been there three times. You're a busy man."

It should have sounded abrupt, but it didn't.

"How long have you known Martyn?"

"Not very long."

"Oh. I see."

"We've been . . ." She hesitated. ". . . close, for about three or four months. I knew him a little before, through work. I work on the same paper."

"Oh, yes. I thought I recognised your name when I first heard it." We stood silently. I looked away. I looked back. Grey eyes stared straight back into mine, and held them, and me, motionless. After a long time she said:

"How very strange."

"Yes," I said.

"I'm going now."

"Goodbye," I said.

She turned, and walked away. Her tall black-suited body seemed to carve its way through the crowded room and disappeared.

A stillness descended upon me. I sighed a deep sigh, as if I had slipped suddenly out of a skin. I felt old, and content. The shock of recognition had passed through my body like a powerful current. Just for a moment I had met my sort, another of my species. We had acknowledged one another. I would be grateful for that, and would let it slip away.

I had been home. For a moment, but longer than most people. It was enough, enough for my lifetime.

Of course, it wasn't enough. But in those early hours I was simply grateful that the moment had occurred. I was like a traveller lost in a foreign land who suddenly hears not just his native tongue, but the local dialect he spoke as a boy. He does not ask whether the voice is that of an enemy or a friend, just rushes towards the sweet sound of home. My soul had rushed to Anna Barton. I believed that in such a private matter between myself and God I could freely let it tumble forwards, without fear of damage to heart or mind, body or life.

It is in that essential misreading that many lives stumble. In the utterly wrong idea that we are in control. That we can choose to go, or stay, without agony. After all, I had only lost my soul privately, at a party, where the others could not see.

She rang me the next day.

"I'm coming to lunch next Sunday. I wanted you to know."

"Thank you."

"Goodbye." The phone went dead.

On Saturday an insanity gripped me. I became convinced that I would die before Sunday. Death would rob me of Sunday. Sunday was now all I wanted. For on Sunday I would sit in the same room as Anna Barton.

On Sunday morning, in what seemed to me the prison of my study, I waited, motionless, for the slamming of the car doors, for the sound of the iron gate on the paving stones, and for the reverberations of the bell, which would first warn me, then summon me, to her presence in my house.

I heard my footsteps on the marble hall as I crossed

to the sitting room, and above the laughter, the metallic click of the handle as I opened the door to join my family, and Anna.

I had delayed them and, as Martyn with his arm around her shoulders said, "Dad, this is Anna," Ingrid whisked us all into the dining room. No one seemed to notice that my breathing had changed.

We all sat down to lunch—Ingrid, Sally, Anna and I, and Martyn.

But of course in reality Ingrid and I sat down with Sally. And Martyn—a different Martyn, tentative, undeniably in love—sat down with Anna.

Anna behaved towards me as any intelligent young woman would, when first meeting the father of her boyfriend. Boyfriend? They must be lovers. Of course they are. They are lovers. Months together. Lovers, of course.

Neither of us mentioned our meeting. Anna concealed even the faintest acknowledgement that such a meeting had ever taken place. Her discretion, at first so soothing in those early minutes, now became the cause of anguish. What kind of woman is such a consummate actress, I thought. How could she be that good?

Her black-dressed body today seemed longer, slightly threatening; frightening even, as she walked from the dining room to the sitting room for coffee. This is the first stage with you, I thought, the first barrier. Watch me, watch, I'm your equal.

"We're thinking of going to Paris for the weekend." Martyn spoke.

"Who?"

"Anna and I, of course."

"It's my favourite city." Anna smiled at Ingrid.

"Oh, I don't really ever enjoy it as much as I hope I will. Something always goes wrong for us in Paris," Ingrid replied.

It was true. Whenever we'd been there handbags were stolen, or we'd had a minor car crash, or Ingrid became ill. She'd fallen out of love with Paris. It was an ideal that had never quite been realised.

I heard all this conversation calmly. I smiled as Ingrid said, "What a nice idea," to Martyn.

The surface remained untroubled, but the ground was beginning to be less firm under my feet. A fault long hidden was being revealed. There was the smallest, briefest tremor, barely worth recording. But the pain that shot through me was so intense, I knew real damage was now being done.

I could not pinpoint what damage, or whether I would recover, or how long it would take. Suffice to know that I was less the man I had been, and more myself . . . a new strange self.

I was now a liar to my family. A woman I had known only for days, to whom I had spoken only a few sentences, watched me betray my wife and my son. And we both knew the other knew. It seemed a bond between us. A concealed truth, that's all a lie is.

Either by omission or commission we never do more than obscure. The truth stays in the undergrowth, waiting to be discovered. But nothing was uncovered that Sunday. The small lie, which was the first betrayal, seemed to sink further and further in the laughter, the wine, and the day.

"Well, what do you think of her?" Ingrid asked me after they left.

"Of Anna?"

"Who else?"

"She's strange."

"Yes, you can see why I'm worried. Martyn's completely out of his depth. It's not just that she's older . . . there's something else. I can't quite put my finger on it, but she's wrong for him. Not that he can see it, of course. He is obviously besotted. Sex, I suppose."

I froze.

"Oh."

"Come on, of course she's sleeping with him. My God, Martyn's had more women than—"

"Than me."

"I should hope so too," said Ingrid as she came to put her arms around me. But the conversation had devastated me. I kissed her gently, and went to my study.

I stood looking out the window into the evening light. Anna was now in my home. She was flitting between rooms, between Ingrid and Martyn and me. Yet nothing had happened, nothing at all. Except, of course, her discovered presence in this world.

She was the split-second experience that changes everything; the car smash; the letter we shouldn't have opened; the lump in the breast or groin; the blinding flash. On my well-ordered stage set the lights were up, and maybe at last I was waiting in the wings.

NINE

"Martyn is coming over for lunch again on Sunday. I think he's got something to tell us."

"What?"

"I hope it's not that he is going to marry Anna, but I fear that it is."

"Marry her?"

"Yes. There was something in his voice. Oh, I don't know. I may be wrong."

"He can't marry her." Why do those we have loved half our lives not know when devastation threatens? How can they simply not know?

"Good God, you sound like a Victorian father. He's over twenty-one. He can do what he likes. I don't like that girl. But I know Martyn. If he wants her, he will have her. He's got your father's determination."

I noticed she did not say mine.

"Well, we must all wait until Sunday," she sighed.

The conversation was over. My thoughts went wildly into battle with each other. I was wounded, defended myself, and fought myself again. Silently, while I pretended to read, on and on the battle raged. I was engulfed by anger and fear. Fear that I would never get control of myself again. That I was now uprooted. And by a storm of such force that even if there was a dim possibility of survival, I would be permanently damaged, permanently weakened.

I had not spoken. I had not touched. I had not possessed. But I had recognised her. And in her, had recognised myself.

I needed to get out of the house and walk. The forced stillness of the room was agony. The pain could only be borne by constant, endless movement.

I touched Ingrid's forehead briefly, and I left the house. How can you not know? Can't you sense, smell, taste disaster waiting in the corners of the house? Waiting at the bottom of the garden.

I was exhausted when I returned. I slept like some heavy animal, uncertain if it can ever rise again.

TEN

"Hello, it's Anna."

I waited quietly. Knowing that in my life there was now an end and a beginning. Not knowing where the beginning would end.

"Where are you? Go to your house. I will be there in an hour," I said. I took the address and put down the phone.

There are hidden enclaves in London of creamy houses, rich with discretion. In the deep oily blackness of the door I watched the outline of my body as I pressed the bell, and waited to enter Anna's small, low, and to me mysterious house.

We made no sound as we moved down the honey-coloured carpet of the hall. We went into her sitting room and lay down on the floor. She flung her arms out, each side of her, and she drew her legs up. I lay down on her. I sank my head on her shoulder. I thought of Christ, still nailed to the cross, which had been laid on the earth. Then with one hand grasping her hair, I entered her.

And there we lay. Not speaking, not stirring until finally I moved my face across hers, and kissed her. And at last the age-old ritual possessed us, and I bit and tore and held her, round and round, as we rose and fell, rose and fell into the wilderness.

Later there would be time for the pain and pleasure lust lends to love. Time for body lines and angles that provoke the astounded primitive to leap delighted from the civilised skin, and tear the woman to him. There would be time for words obscene and dangerous. There would be time for cruel laughter to excite, and for ribbons colourfully to bind limbs to a sickening, thrilling subjugation. There would be time for flowers to put out the eyes, and for silken softness to close the ears. And time also in that dark and silent world for the howl of the lonely man, who had feared eternal exile.

Even if we had never come together again, my life would have been lost in contemplation of the emerging skeleton beneath my skin. It was as though a man's bones broke through the face of the werewolf. Shining with humanity he stalked through his midnight life towards the first day.

We bathed separately. I left alone, without speaking. I walked the long walk home. I stared at Ingrid as she came to greet me, and muttered something about needing to rest for a few hours. I undressed and lay on the bed, and was instantly asleep. I slept through until morning, twelve hours, a kind of death perhaps.

ELEVEN

"Lamb or beef?" asked Ingrid.

"What?"

"Lamb or beef? Sunday lunch, Martyn and Anna."

"Oh. Whatever you think."

"Lamb then. Good, that's settled."

Anna wore white at lunch. It made her appear larger. The suggested innocence of the simple white dress disturbed my other vision of her. It broke my memory of her dark power. She was her other self; the self that dealt carefully with Ingrid, winning at least a grudging respect from her; that gazed openly at Martyn; that calmly spoke to me of food, flowers, and weather; spoke so well, that none could have guessed the truth.

If Ingrid had expected an announcement, there was none forthcoming. They left at four, having refused tea.

"Martyn seemed tense, I thought." Ingrid had begun the ritual post mortem.

"Really. I didn't notice."

"No? Well, he did. He looks at her in a slightly pleading fashion. No doubt who's the lover and the loved there. She seemed a bit less strange. More open, more friendly. Could have been the white dress, I suppose. White always disarms one."

Clever Ingrid, I thought, how you can surprise me.

"Maybe it will all peter out. Oh God, I do hope so. I really couldn't bear the idea of Anna as a daughter-in-law. Could you?"

I paused. The idea seemed too preposterous. An alien concept outside the bounds of possibility. But the question demanded an answer.

"No, I suppose not," I said. We left it there.

TWELVE

I bathed Anna's face, which was raw and damp, and squeezing the sponge let the water run through her hair. For hours, we had fought a battle with the barricades of the body. The battle over, I lay beside her.

"Anna, please . . . talk to me . . . who are you?"

There was a long silence.

"I am what you desire," she said.

"No. That's not what I meant."

"No? But to you, that's what I am. To others I am something else."

"Others? Something else?"

"Martyn. My mother, my father." A long pause. "My family. Friends of my past, my present. It's the same for everyone. For you as well."

"Does Martyn know more? Has he met your parents, your family?"

"No. He asked once. I told him to love me as though he knew me. And if he could not—well then . . ."

"Who are you?"

"Do you have to ask? Oh well, it's simple. My mother's name is Elizabeth Hunter. She is the second wife of Wilbur Hunter, the writer. She lives happily with Wilbur on the West Coast of America. I haven't seen her for two years. This causes me no pain, nor, I believe, does it distress her. We write occasionally. I phone at Christmas, Easter, and birthdays. My father was a diplomat. I travelled a great deal as a child. I went to school in Sussex, spent my holidays anywhere and everywhere. I was not upset when my parents divorced. My father, though apparently distressed at the time of my mother's affair with Wilbur, recovered sufficiently to marry a thirty-five-year-old widow with two children. They have since produced a daughter, Amelia. I visit them occasionally in Devon."

"Were you an only child?"

"No."

I waited.

"I had a brother. Aston. He committed suicide by slashing his wrists and throat in the bathroom of our apartment in Rome. No chance of misinterpretation. It was not a cry for help. No one knew why at the time. I shall tell you. He suffered from an unrequited love of me. I tried to soothe him with my body . . ." She paused, then continued in staccato. "His pain, my foolishness . . . our confusion . . . He killed himself. Understandably. That is my story, simply told. Please do not ask again. I have told you in order to issue a warning. I have been damaged. Damaged people are dangerous. They know they can survive."

For a long time we were silent.

"Why did you say 'understandably' Aston killed himself?"

"Because I understand. I carry that knowledge within me. It is not a treasure that I jealously guard. Simply a story I did not wish to tell, about a boy you have never known."

"That makes you dangerous?"

"All damaged people are dangerous. Survival makes them so."

"Why?"

"Because they have no pity. They know that others can survive, as they did."

"But you have warned me."

"Yes."

"Was that not an act of pity?"

"No. You have gone so far down the road that all warnings are now useless. I will feel better for having told you. Though the timing is wrong."

"And Martyn?"

"Martyn does not need a warning."

"Why not?"

"Because Martyn asks no questions. He is content with me. He allows me my secrets."

"And if he found out the truth?"

"What truth?"

"You and I."

"That truth. There are other truths."

"You seem to ascribe to Martyn qualities of self-sufficiency and maturity I have not noticed."

"No. You haven't noticed."

"And if you are wrong about him?"

"That would be a tragedy."

Of her body I have little to say. It was simply essential. I could not bear the absence of it. Pleasure was an incidental. I threw myself on her, as onto the earth. I forced all parts of her to feed my need and watched her grow larger and more powerful, the more she provided. Hungry, I would hold her at a distance by hair or breast, sick with anger that I could have what I wanted.

And round every meeting with her spun a ribbon of certainty that my life had already ended. It had ended in the split second of my first sight of her.

It was time out of life. Like an acid it ran through all the years behind me, burning and destroying.

THIRTEEN

I had opened a door to a secret vault. Its treasures were immense. Its price would be terrible. I knew that all the defences I had built so carefully—wife, children, home, vocation—were ramparts built on sand. With no knowledge of any other path I had made my journey through the years, seeking and clinging to landmarks of normality.

Did I always know of this secret room? Was my sin basically one of untruthfulness? Or, more likely, one of cowardice? But the liar knows the truth. The coward knows his fear and runs away.

And if I had not met Anna? Ah, what providence for those who suffered such devastation at my hand!

But I did meet Anna. And I had to, and I did open the door, and enter my own secret vault. I wanted my time on earth, now that I had heard the song that sings from head to toe; had known the wildness that whirls the dancers past the gaze of shocked onlookers; had fallen deeper and deeper and had soared higher and higher, into a single reality—the dazzling explosion into self.

What lies are impossible? What trust is so precious? What responsibility is so great that it could deny this single chance in eternity to exist? Alas for me, and for all who knew me, the answer was . . . none.

To be brought into being by another, as I was by Anna, leads to strange, unthought-of needs. Breathing became more difficult without her. I literally felt I was being born. And because birth is always violent, I never looked for, nor ever found, gentleness.

The outer reaches of our being are arrived at through violence. Pain turns into ecstasy. A glance turns into a threat. A challenge deep behind the eye or mouth, that only Anna or I could understand, led us on and on, intoxicated by the power to create our own magnificent universe.

She never cried out. Patiently she suffered the slow torments of my adoration. Sometimes, her limbs locked, impossibly angled, as on a rack of my imagination, stoically she bore my weight. Dark-eyed, motherlike, the timeless creator of the thing that hurt her.

FOURTEEN

"I may have to go to Brussels on Friday." Ingrid and I were having a pre-dinner drink in the drawing room.

"Oh, no! Why? I hoped we could go to Hartley to see Father. I felt like a nice peaceful weekend in the country. I thought you might have been able to come up, on Sunday at least." Ingrid sounded pained.

"I'm sorry, really sorry. I'd have liked to go to Hartley. But there's an absolutely key meeting I've got to get to. And while I'm there, George Broughton has arranged two lunches. And a dinner. With our Dutch counterparts. You go to Hartley. You and Edward always have such a nice time together. I don't know of a father and daughter who are closer."

Ingrid laughed. She and Edward really did have the most extraordinary ease with each other. I often felt like an outsider. And Hartley was beautiful. Edward had bought it early in his career and taken his young bride to live there.

"I'll ask Sally if she can come."

"That's a good idea."

"Maybe she can bring this new boyfriend. I don't know if it's serious. He's quite a nice chap. Nick Robinson's son."

"How did she meet him?"

"He's an assistant producer at the television company."
Sally had recently left publishing to work in television.

"Well, Nick's a gentleman. Ask Sally and her chap.
You'll all have a wonderful time."

"Martyn is going to Paris, of course, with Anna. God,
that's looking more and more serious."

My back was to her.

"Where are they staying?"

"Oh, at some place Anna knows. Frightfully expensive and very trendy, I gather. L'Hôtel. Yes, I think that's
what it's called."

I drank my whisky. So easy, so easy. Anna had refused
to tell me. I hadn't spoken to Martyn for a week.

"Anna has money, you know." Ingrid spoke disapprovingly.

"Has she?"

"It's quite a lot evidently. Left to her by her grandfather, I gather. That's how she can afford that mews
house she lives in, and her very expensive car."

"Well, Martyn's not exactly penniless. And he's got
the trust fund set up by my father and Edward."

"Yes I know. But Anna's the kind of girl who would
have been better off without money."

"What on earth do you mean?"

"Money does things to a woman."

"Really. What? And don't forget you had a lot of
money when we married."

"Ah, but I'm not Anna. Whatever people say nowadays, marriage requires a woman to at least act out a certain kind of dependence. Money is sometimes the currency
of that dependence. In a subtle woman, her economic inde-

pendence is shaded, possibly hidden altogether." She had the grace to laugh. "Seriously, that girl has a fierce nature."

"I don't know why we keep calling her a girl. She's a woman over thirty."

"Yes. And she looks it. She is very sophisticated, confident. But there is something of the girl, something girlish, still there."

"She seems to fascinate you," I said.

Ingrid looked at me.

"Not you? Doesn't she fascinate you? She suddenly arrives in Martyn's life. Over thirty, unmarried—as far as we know—rich, sophisticated, and she has an affair with Martyn. After a relationship of only three to four months Martyn is thinking of marriage. Martyn! Martyn the Lothario!"

"You've said that before. I see no signs of it. I'm sure this affair will be like all of the others. One Sunday he will turn up for lunch with another blonde. Come to think of it, before Anna they were all blondes." Anger and fear distorted my voice. Though I tried to sit quietly I had to move towards the window.

"You are blind. For an intelligent man."

"Thank you."

"Even occasionally a brilliant man."

"Oh, thank you again, madam."

Ingrid laughed.

"You never see what's in front of you. Martyn's sweet racy days with the blondes are over. For all his experience, he has been stunned by this girl. He certainly means to marry her. I'm positive of that. What her intentions are, well, they are as much of a mystery as everything else about her."

"I think you're wrong. If Martyn is in love, he's still very young to marry."

"For heaven's sake, he's twenty-five."

"Well, it's quite young."

"We were married younger than that."

"All right then. So he's not too young. It's just that Anna's not right for him. I'm certain of that."

"Well, we're both certain of that. It's not a happy situation, is it? We don't like her. Martyn loves her."

She looked at me, quizzically.

"Of course, I assume you don't like her. But come to think of it, you've never really voiced an opinion . . . a serious opinion . . . have you?"

I looked her straight in the face.

"I suppose I haven't thought much about her. I'm sorry."

"You had better start thinking now, my dear. Or before you know where you are, and perhaps before you've made up your mind about her, she'll be your daughter-in-law."

She looked carefully at me. I tried to smile. Surely something must show of the struggle inside? But my face can have betrayed little.

"Think about it," she said. "I feel you should talk to Martyn soon—man to man. Think about what to say."

"Yes, I will."

"Perhaps in between your meetings in Brussels. It's easier to think things through away from familiar surroundings."

The conversation was over.

"I'll leave for Hartley on Thursday evening, if that's

all right with you. Sally can get the train on Friday night."

"Yes. I'm leaving first thing on Friday morning."

"Let's have dinner then. No more talk of children and their romances. Let's plan our summer holiday."

FIFTEEN

The desperation that compelled me to leave Brussels, and to take the night train to Paris, was driven by a terror that I might never see her again. I had to see her. In order to live, I knew I had to see her.

And yet, did I not plan this? I had tricked Ingrid into giving me the name of their hotel. Was I really consumed by forces beyond my control? Or was I colluding in some needed, longed-for destruction? The wheels of the train, rhythmically grinding the miles from Brussels into oblivion, had the implacability of some great machine of fate.

Paris seemed to have the morning air of a village that is preparing for a fete. Each person knew how to play his part, and when to begin. I sat in a café, and had coffee and croissants. Then, as if drawing a map in my head, I walked around the streets close to ‚L'Hôtel. I watched and waited, carefully noted the time. I swore to myself that I would not phone until nine.

I remembered Anna saying she would make all the arrangements. So I gambled.

"Madame Barton, s'il vous plaît."

"Un moment. Ne quittez pas."

The receptionist put me through.

"Hello. Go to the end of the street. Turn into Rue Jacques Callot, just off Rue de Seine."

"Oui, bien. Merci."

I put the phone down.

It had been so simple. I was trembling with joy and longing. Lines from childhood sang in my head, 'All a-wonder and a wild, wild longing.'

My maniac's face as I walked from the booth startled a passerby. I tried to compose my features. I put my hand to my jaw and remembered I was unshaven, unwashed. What had been all a-wonder and a wild, wild longing? I felt like something from the wild. And oh, the longing, longing!

I leaned against a wall, and looked down a side street for some hiding place in which to hold her. I must hold her.

At nine-thirty I saw her head flash for a second, between the laughing faces of a family group. She stepped off the pavement, overtook them, and ran to me. I pulled her down the alleyway and pushed her towards the wall. I threw myself upon her. My arms spread-eagled on the wall, my legs apart so that all my body could grind itself as hard as possible onto hers. My mouth and face bit and scraped her lip, her skin, her eyelids. I licked her hairline. I let a hand drop from the wall, and holding her by her hair, gasped, "I have to have you." She slipped her skirt up, was naked underneath, and in a second I was inside her. "I know, I know," she whispered. It was over in minutes. I fell away from her.

Someone rounded the corner. They moved to the other side of the small alley. I had been lucky again. As we held each other, Anna and I had the appearance of lovers locked in an embrace. In Paris that day, I was forgiven.

She arranged her dress, smoothing the crumpled skirt. Then from her bag she took her knickers, and smiling a sudden, girlish smile, she slid them on.

I looked at her, and cried, "Oh Anna, Anna. I just had to, I just had to."

"I know," she whispered again, "I know."

I wept. It occurred to me that I could not remember ever crying as an adult. It had simply never happened.

"I must go back now," she said to me.

"Yes. Yes, of course. How did you get out? What did you say?"

"I explained to you once before. Martyn doesn't question me. I said I wanted to have a little walk. Alone." She smiled.

"What power you have!"

"I suppose I do. But you both came to me. I didn't search you out."

"Didn't you? You didn't stop us either."

"Could I stop you in this?"

"No."

"I must go."

"I thought you said he never questioned you."

"Yes. It's a kind of pact. Maybe even a bargain. I try not to abuse it. Goodbye."

"Anna. What are you going to do today? Where are you going?"

"I must go now. I really must. Martyn and I will come home on Monday evening. You must not stay in Paris. I know what you will do . . . you will follow us. Go home. Please."

"I will. Just tell me."

"Why?"

"I can think of you, and where you are."

"And who I'm with."

"Not yet. I have not thought about that yet. I simply can't see past you."

"You know, I think you've never seen very much at all. Ever."

She turned and walked away. She didn't look back. I slid to the pavement like some drunken vagabond. I crouched there with my head in my hands. At the end of the alleyway I glimpsed the other Paris, now having lost its morning softness, glide elegantly by.

Our sanity depends essentially on a narrowness of vision—the ability to select the elements vital to survival, while ignoring the great truths. So the individual lives his daily life, without due attention to the fact that he has no guarantee of tomorrow. He hides from himself the knowledge that his life is a unique experience, which will end in the grave; that at every second, lives as unique as his start and end. This blindness allows a pattern of living to hand itself on, and few who challenge this pattern survive. With good reason. All the laws of life and society would seem irrelevant, if each man concentrated daily on the reality of his own death.

And so, in the great moment of my life, my vision extended only to Anna. What had, as she said, been a life of singular blindness, now necessitated the ruthless obliteration from my vision of Martyn, Ingrid, and Sally. They seemed but shadows.

Martyn's reality had been most brutally stamped out. He was a figure in a canvas, over which another had been painted.

SIXTEEN

I keep always ready and packed a bag, with shirt, underpants, socks, extra tie, and shaving kit.

My career, which often demanded sudden overnight departures, made my "emergency bag" a necessity. Oblivious to it on my journey, and in my minutes with Anna, I now picked it up from the gutter. In a men's lavatory I repaired my outer self.

As I looked in the mirror, my unshaven face and sunken eyes seemed appropriate to me. This is someone I recognise, I thought. I felt a great joy. As I shaved, I felt my mask less tight upon me. I was certain that someday soon, it would slip away entirely. But not yet.

I rang L'Hôtel.

"*Madame Barton, s'il vous plaît, je pense que c'est chambre . . .*"

"*Ah, chambre dix. Madame Barton n'est-pas là. Elle est partie.*"

"*Pour la journée?*"

"*Non, elle a quitté l'hôtel.*"

It was as I thought.

She must have left immediately. Anna, woman of action! I smiled.

I went to a bookshop, and waited for exactly one hour. I rang the hotel.

"*Oui, L'Hôtel réception . . .*"

"Do you speak English?"

"Yes, certainly."

"I would like to book a room. Do you have one?"

"For how long?"

"I find I must unexpectedly stay in Paris for just one night."

"Yes, we have a room."

"Good. I have sentimental memories of your hotel. Do you by any chance have room ten free?"

"Yes, it's free."

"Marvellous, I will come after lunch."

I gave my name, details of how I would pay, and hung up.

Will, will. I remembered my father's old motto. I felt triumphant. I thought of the night's journey, and of how I had succeeded in seeing Anna. I had undertaken a dangerous endeavour. I had won. I had the will. I had the luck. I remembered Napoleon's main requirement of his generals—luck.

I was lucky now.

Suddenly, I felt ravenously hungry. Appetite and sensuality flooded through me. I made a reservation at Laurent, and having been ushered to a quiet table overlooking the garden, I ordered lunch. "*Millefeuille de saumon,* followed by . . . *poulet façon maison.*" I ordered a bottle of Meursault. I ate with a kind of rapture. The wine looked and tasted like liquid gold. The pastry seemed to explode gently in my mouth, as the salmon slipped from its crevices. It was as though I were eating for the first time. I was glad I was alone. I needed time, and distance from Anna, so that I could lose myself in memories of the morning.

Pale honey slices of chicken, in an amber-coloured sauce; a salad of whitened green that gleamed; creamy coloured cheese; the deep red of port; colours so intense, and shades so subtle. I slipped softly into the world of the senses. A body that could stretch out fully to imprison, release, restrain, or devour its prey, could now also eat food the way food should be eaten.

I was sick with pleasure when I entered the room Anna and Martyn had so swiftly vacated that morning.

I had been led quietly up the strange curve of the staircase, where circular floors and secret rooms ascended to a magnificent dome.

I had no sentimental knowledge of L'Hôtel. I had heard of it, of course. But the room shocked me. It had a heavy air of sensuality. Anna's choice was a room for lovers. Blue and gold brocade curtains, a chaise longue of red velvet, dark golden mirrors, a circular bathroom, small, windowless.

Anna had chosen this hotel for Martyn and herself. I closed, then locked the door.

Lust and rage engulfed me. I lay on their bed. Now in its pristine perfection, it denied any other occupant but me. The chaise longue obsessed me. Maybe there, I thought. Maybe there. She doesn't like bed. No. No, it's you who doesn't like bed. You don't know her. She answered your needs, that's all. When have you really talked to her, you fool? I became naked, throwing clothes on floor and chairs. In a rage, I lay on the wine velvet chaise longue and slowly, methodically, and with little pleasure I sent spurts of semen into its blood-coloured beauty.

Then, as this strange day of triumph and defeat drew to a close, from the evening shadows Paris the magnificent arose. Powerful and implacable, its majesty seemed to underscore my own frailty and weakness.

I moved on all fours like some heavy animal from my velvet world, and fell onto the bed. In a dreamfall of colours—the green of Anna's dress, the flash of black as she slipped on her knickers, the liquid gold of the wine, and the sunlit pales of the millefeuille and salmon, the violent blood red of the chaise longue, and the sombre darkness of the blue brocade curtains—the day slipped away. And with it departed the man I used to be. He seemed, as I fell further down this kaleidoscope of the day's colours, to slip into the Paris night, like a black shadow, or a ghost.

I closed my eyes. A childhood terror came back to me. When you fall in dreams, you die. If you hit the ground.

SEVENTEEN

It took a while for the L'Hôtel switchboard to connect me to Hartley.

"Hello, Edward. How are you?"

"Marvellous, my dear boy. It's such a pleasure to have Ingrid and Sally here. They don't come to Hartley often enough. Neither do you, I may say."

"I know, I know. I miss it."

"Well, you're very busy. Sally's new young man, Jonathan, is here. Nick Robinson's boy, you know. Only Labour chap I can take to."

I thought this might have been because Nick Robinson was one of the few Labour "chaps" with a public school background, and an impeccable Shires heritage.

"I knew Nick's mother, you know. Could never understand Jesse Robinson's son becoming a Labour MP. Ah, well. You want to talk to Ingrid, I expect?"

"Yes. If she's around."

"She's in the garden. Hold on a moment."

"Hello, darling. How's Brussels?"

"Deadly. Actually, I had to dash to Paris for a morning meeting. I'm catching a plane back tonight."

"No chance of seeing Martyn and Anna then?"

"No." I paused. "I thought of calling them to invite them for a slap-up meal, but there isn't time. I just won't bother them at all."

"Probably right," said Ingrid. "A weekend in Paris is for romance, I suppose. Fathers are not the most welcome of dinner companions for young lovers."

"No. I suppose not."

"Such a pity. I'd be quite pleased to see Martyn in love. If only it wasn't with Anna. Anyway, enough of that."

"You having a lovely time there? Weather good?"

"Just lovely. Every time I come back to Hartley, I seem to love it more and more. I thought of Mother a lot today. Walking with Sally reminded me so much of my walks with her. I suppose we were never really that close. But yesterday I missed her, rather badly. I wish you'd been here."

"So do I."

"Do you?"

"Yes. Yes, of course."

"Jonathan is a rather nice young man."

"So Edward says."

"Safe journey, darling. Would you like me to come back earlier?"

"No. Absolutely not. You enjoy your few days at Hartley. I'll ring you tomorrow."

"Bye, darling."

"Bye-bye."

It's so hideously easy, I thought. To tell her I was in Paris was risky, I could easily have concealed it. The new and strange shape I was assuming was hardening each day. The facile liar, the violent lover, the betrayer, would allow no return journey. My path was clear. I knew I was on a headlong rush to destruction. But I was certain I could control and plan each step of the way—with a mixture of restrained joy and cold deception that I began to find intoxicating. I felt not a shred of pity for anyone. That was the essence of my power.

I bathed and changed. I brushed a flaking mosaic of semen from the chaise longue. Having paid the bill I left for Charles de Gaulle. I wondered what I would say if I came across Anna and Martyn? Anna could be relied upon to dissemble. Could I deliver a perfect performance? Would she despise me if I failed? My love token is a garland of lies, I thought. She has crowned me with lies since the day I met her. But in the centre of my crown, like a diamond, rests the only truth that matters to me: Anna.

Luck stayed with me, clearing my path. With an almost delicate ease, I left Paris in a triumph of moral degradation.

EIGHTEEN

"Your son is on the line, sir."

"Put him through."

"Hello, Dad. Sorry to disturb you in your office."

"Martyn, how are you?"

"Great. We've just got back from Paris."

"Nice time?"

"Well, yes. Anna was a little unwell, so we came back early."

"Unwell?"

"Yes. Stomach cramps, violent headache. She went to see her old doctor. Then we left."

"How is she now?"

"Oh, she's fully recovered. Thanks for asking. I rather appreciate you always being so . . . sensitive . . . about her. Mum doesn't really like Anna."

"Oh, I'm sure she does. Anna is an interesting girl."

"I think that's what Mum doesn't like. She'd like me to be with another version of Sally, I suppose. You know, twenty-two, very English, et cetera, et cetera."

"Not very flattering to your sister, all this."

"Oh, Dad, I love Sally. You know what I mean."

"Yes. Yes I do."

"I know you're busy, Dad, but I just wanted to tell you I've been offered a job on the Sunday ——." He mentioned one of the country's leading newspapers. "I'm Deputy Political Editor."

"I'm impressed. Congratulations."

"I'd rather like to take you and Mum out to dinner. To celebrate. Thursday possible?"

I hesitated. "Yes, probably. I may have to leave early to get back to the House."

"That's fine. So Thursday at Luigi's. I'm inviting Sally too. And that new chap of hers. So you see, brotherly feelings are still strong!"

He laughed, and rang off.

"Alistair Stratton on the line, sir."

"Just hold him a moment, can you, Jane?"

I needed to recover. Not only from the sudden shock of talking to Martyn, but from the conversation itself, which had disturbed me. I was not the only person who was changing. Martyn the man was emerging more strongly.

"Put Alistair through," I sighed. The day then trapped me in its iron bars of phone calls and meetings, letters to read, letters to write, decisions to make, promises to break. And underneath its structure lay a growing sense of alarm, and a sudden gnawing fear of Martyn.

NINETEEN

We were an impressive-looking group as we entered the restaurant.

Edward had joined us. In his dark blue suit, he had the air of a man who knows that his presence enhances every gathering.

Ingrid was in subtle shades of grey, understated, elegant; certain that she was, as always, perfectly dressed.

Sally exuded a sort of 'feet on the ground' decency. It would always defeat her mother's efforts to change her English-rose prettiness into something more soignée. A daughter's penchant for Laura Ashley effectively puts paid to any mother's attempts to encourage sophistication. I had been a frequent onlooker during teenage battles. I saw with pleasure that Sally, the woman, had kept her sartorial loyalties.

Her boyfriend was blond and sporty looking. He wore a suit that observed the convention of matching jacket and trousers, while managing somehow to mock the tradition, with a zig-zag pattern of blacks and greys.

I studied each person slowly, carefully, in order to avoid turning my attention to Anna and Martyn. It was possible to stand close to Anna and yet not look at her. It was even possible to receive a fleeting kiss on the cheek from Anna and still not see her.

Martyn took charge of the seating. I was on Anna's right. "No couples tonight," joked Martyn. Sally to my right sat beside Martyn and Ingrid, then Sally's boyfriend and Edward. I gave a sideways glance at Anna, who seemed to be wearing something in dark blue. It made her hair look even darker. A line from an old song came back to me, 'A dark girl dressed in blue.'

We ordered. The guests carefully and silently examined prices before decisions were taken.

"Well, that's over," said Edward. "What a pleasure to have been invited, Martyn. And congratulations on your new job."

We all raised our glasses to Martyn.

"Anna, you're also a journalist."

"Yes."

"Did you and Martyn meet at work?"

"Yes, we did."

"How nice," said Edward, glancing coolly at her. He had a 'Don't be too clever with me, young woman' look in his eye.

"Do you like your work?"

"Yes, I do."

"Why?"

"It suits me," said Anna.

"How?"

"This sounds like the Inquisition, Grandpa."

"I'm so sorry. Was I being rude?"

"Never," said Martyn. "Anna's an excellent journalist."

"Clearly you are too," said Edward. "Do you think it's for life, this work of yours?"

"Yes. I like the world of newspapers. It's exciting—copy dates, seeing my stuff in the paper."

"Hoping people will read it," offered Sally.

"People do read it, Sally. I know exactly where I'm going." He looked at Anna as he spoke.

I had to turn away quickly. For a second I had seen the passion in his eyes.

"Father, Martyn has always been certain that journalism was what he wanted."

"Yes. But then people can change direction quite late, can't they?" Edward looked at me.

"Politics you mean," said Martyn. "God, no, I don't want to be a politician. It wouldn't suit me, Grandpa. I leave that to you and Dad."

"Oh, but it would suit you. You are articulate, very handsome, yes, and very clever."

"And very, very uninterested," said Martyn emphatically. "I want the kind of freedom I couldn't find in political life, always toeing the party line."

"Well now," said Edward, "what about the line of the chap who owns the paper?"

"Accurate reporting of an event is not normally at risk. It's only in the leader that any proprietorial bias is seriously taken into account," said Martyn.

"What do you think about that, Anna?" asked Sally's boyfriend suddenly.

"Oh, I'm just an observer," said Anna. "I observe carefully. I write truthfully, exactly what I have observed. It gives me pleasure."

"Observation is Anna's strength," said Martyn. "She misses nothing . . . nothing. I don't know anyone more acute than Anna."

I sensed Anna's bowed head. I looked at Ingrid and saw her eyes narrow. Then a look of resignation passed over her face. Our eyes met. 'She's got our son,' they seemed to say. And more, I thought, and more.

"Now, young man, let's turn the third degree on you. What's Nick Robinson's son doing working for TV? What is this generation of media slaves up to? We've had newspapers and the delights of the observer's position. Let's hear it for television. What's its attraction for you?"

"Power, eventually, I hope."

"Power! Well now. That's something I can understand. How are you going to get power, young man?"

"Information . . . can change the world. I don't think politicians . . . I mean . . ." He stumbled in a minefield of potential insult. "Well, I don't think they can really change the way people think about life, and the world. Whereas television can, and does. I really want in time . . . I really want to make feature programmes . . . about social issues which . . ."

"That used to be the province of the artist. To change lives and souls through art."

Everyone looked at me, except Anna, who, I sensed, did not move her head.

"Good heavens," said Sally. "What a serious group we are. Art, politics, the media. This is meant to be a celebration party for Martyn."

Edward laughed. "I've had such a good time putting all you young people through your paces. I'd like you all to come to Hartley for the weekend of the twentieth . . . for my birthday. Just the family, and the about-to-be family." Edward smiled at Anna and Jonathan.

"How marvellous. You can go, darling, can't you?" asked Ingrid.

"Possibly. I'll have to check."

"Anna?"

"I think so. Yes, thank you."

Sally and Jonathan agreed. The thought of a weekend with Anna and Martyn in Hartley opened a world of terror and possibilities, and joy.

The meal meandered slowly through to a teasing sweetness at the end. I had survived close on three hours without by as much as a murmur betraying myself, or Anna.

Perhaps the devil stood behind me, and delivered me successfully to evil.

TWENTY

"I felt proud this evening. Content. I felt the power of being a mother. 'Look on my works, oh ye mighty,'" Ingrid sighed.

We were in the car. The evening had ended properly, with manly insistence from Martyn that the bill was for him, and admiring acquiescence from his father and grandfather.

"Did you feel like the paterfamilias?"

"Mmm."

"It's very satisfying, isn't it?"

"Very."

"We are quiet people, you and I. We suit each other. I feel very happy tonight. You make me very happy. Do I tell you that often enough? Perhaps not. But I hope you know. I don't see many happy marriages around. I'm very grateful for mine . . . and for you."

I smiled.

"It's been a long time. You and me," I said.

"Yes. Two lovely children, a contented marriage. It's almost too good to be true. But it is true. It's so substantially true. I like what I felt tonight, the substance of it. I felt I could almost reach out and touch it. Happiness. The right kind of happiness."

"Is there a right kind?"

"Yes. Yes, I think so. I've always felt so. I've always known what I wanted. A husband, children, peace and progress. I'm very proud of your career, you know. Very, very proud. I'm not ambitious for myself . . . I've always had money . . . but I do my bit, don't I? The constituency and the charities, the dinner parties." She laughed. "Do I fulfil my role, my public role?"

"Indeed you do. You always have."

"So here we are then. It's a very, very good place in our lives. I feel the future, your future, our future, could be very interesting. When I was at Hartley, Daddy said how highly thought of you are. He says you're regarded as a 'coming man.' Even though I say so myself, you are rather perfect, aren't you? Terrific on television. Decent, very intelligent, with a wonderful wife"—she giggled— "and two utterly charming children. Perfect. It's all perfect. Except for Anna. She is a very, very strange girl, don't you think?" Ingrid was suddenly alert.

"Why?"

"I like quiet people, I can't stand super-friendly, outgoing types . . . like that Rebecca girl he had for a while. But Anna's quietness is more mysterious. She is almost sinister. I mean, what do we know about her? She met Martyn through work. She's thirty-three, and very well off. It's ridiculous. For example, what did she do all those years before Martyn?"

"I don't know." I glanced studiously into my mirror. I could not be tripped. No 'How did you know?' errors in this potential interrogation.

"You see! We know nothing. This girl may very well become our daughter-in-law, and we know nothing about her."

I breathed deeply. Slowly now, I said to myself, slowly.

"Martyn has had so many girlfriends, Ingrid. Anna is just another one. Maybe a bit more serious. But marriage? No, I don't think so."

"Well, you are utterly wrong, I'm afraid. He mentioned his trust fund the other day, when he was arranging the dinner. He comes into his capital when he marries. Remember, his promotion to a national newspaper gives him great confidence. Can't you see that boy is seriously planning his future? God knows, you can't stop a man in love having what he wants. If Anna wants him, she's going to be his wife. Of course he most certainly wants her. I think as parents we should at least try to get to know her better. And we should find out more about her past. Have you questioned Martyn yet? I've tried. It's quite difficult. He says he knows all he needs to know. However, I got some information from him about her parents. He says they're very respectable. Her father was in the diplomatic service. The parents divorced, and her mother remarried. An American writer, I gather. Her father has a second family too."

"That doesn't sound too terrible, does it?"

"No, but there's something else, I'm sure. For example, has Anna been married before?"

"How extraordinary. I never thought of that."

"Well, you've hardly given her any thought at all, have you?"

"No. I suppose not." I breathed slowly, determinedly.

"Men! Well, think about it. She's thirty-three, it's perfectly possible. In fact, it's surprising if she hasn't been. Maybe she has children. You never know nowadays. Think of Beatrice, her children stayed with their father in Italy."

"I'm certain there are no children." The doctor in me spoke.

"What? You know nothing about her, but you're certain she has no children."

"Oh, I don't know, just a very strong guess. Come on, let's have a nightcap at home."

She put her arms around me when we got to our room. "Sorry. I shouldn't have let Anna spoil a lovely evening. Did I tell you how very impressive you looked this evening?" She kissed me. "I love you," she whispered. "Darling, let's go to our lovely bed. I can see that look in your eyes—I like it."

And so we lay in bed. A man whose eyes could deceive a wife of nearly thirty years, and a wife who after nearly thirty years could be so deceived. Our practised movements were as pleasant as an old remembered song of long ago. But even as I surrendered to those final shudders that are all and nothing, it was, I knew, a final defeat for Ingrid in a battle she did not know she waged. And it was a triumph for Anna, who had not even fought.

'I cannot and will not do this again.' That was my last thought as Ingrid drifted dreamily to sleep in my arms.

TWENTY-ONE

"Hello, Dad." It was Martyn on the line.

"Martyn. Thank you for last night and congratulations again."

"Oh, thanks. You were very quiet. Working too hard? I know you're heading one of those committees—I gather it's getting close to recommendation time."

"How do you know?"

He laughed. "I can't reveal my sources."

"I suppose I'd better be more careful than usual now. Even secret smiles are out of the question."

"Absolutely. Journalist first, son second!" He laughed. "Oh yes, I'd spill all your secrets for the chance of a scoop."

"Aha! I've been warned!" I entered into the spirit of the thing.

"Dad, I want to ask you something about my trust fund."

"Yes."

"Can I talk to Charles Longdon about it? And to David, he's the other trustee, isn't he?" He mentioned a cousin of Ingrid's.

"Yes. Why do you need to talk to them?"

There was a long pause. "I . . . oh, I don't know. Plans, you know. It's about time I examined all my financial affairs. Properly. Don't you think?"

"Well, you know the trust doesn't come to you until you marry?" I spoke slowly, staring unseeing out the window.

"Yes, I know that. Still, I'd like to talk to them about it. Just wanted you and Edward to know. I didn't want to go behind your back, or anything."

"No. No, of course. I don't mind. Go ahead."

The call was over. No mention of Anna. Martyn would make his own decisions. There would be no consultation with anyone. Just as it should be. And his plans were very clear. He meant to ask Anna to marry him. She would refuse him, of course. What then? How would he react?

And what of Anna and me? We never spoke of the future. We never even spoke of the present.

TWENTY-TWO

"Anna."

"Come in."

"Was it difficult getting away?"

"No. Do you want a drink?"

"I'd like a glass of red wine."

We were in Anna's house. She sat opposite me. She put her glass down, slowly and deliberately, on a side table.

"You are going to start a conversation I don't think I want to have. So it might be better to finish our wine, and part for today."

"No." Something in my voice may have told her I must be heard, because she replied, "All right."

"I must know that you will be in my life forever. I must know that."

"Why?"

"Because I must know that I can look at you, listen to you, breathe you, be inside you. I have got to know that. I can't go back to being . . . almost dead. It's not possible for me. That is how I was. There can be no 'after Anna' in my life."

"That's because you can't envisage it. But there can be. It's just that it's a life after—"

"I don't want it. It's not going to happen." I got up from my chair and stood in front of her. Perhaps there was something threatening in my movements. There was a tense silence between us. I moved away.

"I think Martyn is going to ask you to marry him."

"Do you?"

"It will be very sad for him. But it will lead to a resolution of this terrible situation."

"What will be sad for Martyn?"

A marble coldness, the coldness of deep shock, enveloped me. Her words seemed frozen in the air. As if in a dream I heard her say, "I like Martyn. We have a very happy time together. I can build a real life with him. I may very well say yes. Martyn is far too intelligent to have gone this far without at least the chance of an acceptance."

There are words we never dream we will utter.

"You are considering marrying Martyn?"

"Considering. Yes."

"You would marry my son?"

There are answers we never dream we will hear.

"Possibly. I warned you at the beginning. I told you to take care."

"Damaged people are dangerous. They know they can survive."

"Yes. You remember. You can have what you want of me forever. I want what you want. We can continue for all our lives, together. Lives can be arranged like that. If I married Martyn, think how easy it would be. We could see each other all the time. I could entwine myself around you like ivy round a tree. I recognised my ruler. The moment I saw you, I surrendered."

Her voice almost sang the words as she moved about the room.

"But I also want Martyn. I want his life to share. He is my normality. We will be like any young couple setting out together. It's right, it's normal."

She spoke the word 'normal' as though it were a benediction.

"It's what I want. I want to marry Martyn. Be happy for me. You will have no less of me. You will have more of me. Yes. More, constantly more. Listen to me. I don't want to marry you. Oh, I know you haven't even thought about it. But you will, you will. You will start agonising over Ingrid. You will start making plans. Listen to me. Martyn would never, ever forgive you. He would be lost to you forever. Sally would be dreadfully harmed. I would be the centre of a terrible scandal. And you, you would be destroyed. And for what? So that we could have a domestic life together. It would be a nonsense. We were not made for that. No, we are made for what it is that we have. The constant satisfaction of our need for each other."

"Perhaps you are mad, Anna. Perhaps that's the reason for what you're saying. Oh, God . . ."

"I am totally sane."

"When did you work all this out?"

"I haven't 'worked it out,' as you put it, in some cold-blooded fashion. Things happened. I met Martyn—we started our affair. It became more than either of us could have imagined. And then you turned a secret corner in your life, and I was there. I had no control over these two events. I did not know I was going to meet Martyn. I did not know I would meet you.

"But I always recognise the forces that will shape my

life. I let them do their work. Sometimes they tear through my life like a hurricane. Sometimes they simply shift the ground under me, so that I stand on different earth, and something or someone has been swallowed up. I steady myself, in the earthquake. I lie down, and let the hurricane pass over me. I never fight. Afterwards I look around me, and I say, 'Ah, so this at least is left for me. And that dear person has also survived.' I quietly inscribe on the stone tablet of my heart the name which has gone forever. The inscription is a thing of agony. Then I start on my way again. Now you and Martyn, and indeed Ingrid and Sally, are in the eye of a storm I did not create. What power is mine, and what responsibility?"

"But you spoke of surrender, of being ruled."

"It is my surrender that makes you ruler. You must accept this. If you fight, or try to change the pieces on the board, or to design a scenario more acceptable to you, you will be lost. Kneel down before me now, and I shall be your slave."

And so I did, in the room in which I had first lain with her. Is it important which way I tried to take her? Which entrance? And whether with tongue or hand or penis? Did she lie or stand? Was her back to me or to the wall? Were her hands free or bound? Did she see my face or not?

Tales of ecstasy are endless tales of failure. For always comes separation. And the journey towards the essential, fleeting unity begins again.

Afterwards I left, a powerless ruler. Anna lay in some strange awkwardness on the table, silent, glistening, and still.

I have no sense of place. Only once, in L'Hôtel in

Paris, did the shapes and colours that make a room pleasing to the eye enter my consciousness.

That afternoon, however, as I closed the door, the room seemed to paint itself on my mind's eye. A dark swirl of rich green lay against pale beige walls. The velvet softly touched the glass windows which looked out over a tiny, walled garden. The wooden floor reflected darker beiges, and lighter browns that shone in spaces empty of furniture.

The chairs and sofas were covered in an old brocade, which suggested all the shades of autumn, and no one colour. The hardbacked chairs, which had fallen on the floor as we struggled to the carved cold darkness of the table where she now lay, were cushioned in the same shade of green velvet as the curtains. From the walls huge angular faces, half in shadow, of a man and a woman and a child, gazed at each other and at us, with a malevolence the painter cannot have intended. Bookcases, containing only hardbacks and some first editions, stood either side of a stone fireplace, bare of ornament.

I can look at this room forever, I thought. I will always have it with me. Until I die.

If you had seen me on television that night, standing in for my Minister, answering questions with my practised mixture of intelligence and charm, you would not have guessed that my inner eye gazed at my painting. As though it held the secret of my life.

TWENTY-THREE

My Lord,

Sometimes we need a map of the past. It helps us to understand the present, and to plan the future.

As you left you gazed at me and at everything, as though you were seeing it for the last time.

After I had bathed and put the room together again, I decided to stay at home, to write to tell you why I am so certain that I am doing the right thing. I want to take away this mystery.

I say little about myself because it matters to virtually no one. My particular past is important only perhaps to you, and to Martyn.

I'm sorry. But I must bring him into this letter. I now feel certain we shall marry.

You need this explanation more than he does. Martyn, as I said once before, is quite fearless in his feelings about me. He accepts, without, of course, knowing why, that a part of me remains forever closed to him. He can handle disappearances, separations, and silences in a way that you can't. You know him so little. Believe me, he is remarkable.

You both could understand my little story. Only you need to hear it.

I travelled a great deal as a child. The process of endlessly starting in fresh schools, with new friends and strange languages, draws the members of a family very close indeed. The family becomes the only constant. We were a close family. My mother certainly loved my father in those early days. Aston and I were all-in-all to each other. We told each other everything. We shared each other's problems. We became an invincible duo against every childhood adversity.

You cannot imagine what such a closeness is like. When it starts so early you see the world always, and in every way, through twinned souls. When we were very small we shared a bedroom. We fell asleep to each other's breathing, and with each other's last words in our ears. In the mornings we gazed at each other and at each new day—together. Whether we were in Egypt, the Argentine, or finally in Europe, it simply didn't matter. The world was Aston and me.

Aston was much cleverer than me, academically clever. Oh, I did perfectly well. But he was brilliant.

My father, to his credit, had resisted sending him away to school when he was seven. He decided in our teens, however, that it was essential we both go to boarding school in England.

My boarding school was a perfectly proper one in Sussex. In the beginning I was miserable without Aston. But I adjusted.

Aston, however, seemed to change. He was always quiet, but now he withdrew more and more into his studies. He seemed to make no friends. His letters to me were full of sadness.

I told my father that I was worried about Aston. The school, when my father talked to them, put it down to a difficult period of adjustment.

Our first holidays (we missed each other at Half Term) started strangely. I ran to Aston, my arms and legs ready to grasp and hold him. He put his hand over my face, and pushed me away, saying:

"I've missed you too much. I don't want to look at you. I don't want to touch you. It's too much. Tomorrow, I'll look at you." And he went to his room.

My father was away. Mother put Aston's non-appearance at dinner down to over-excitement.

His door was locked when I went upstairs. I heard him call to Mother when she knocked, "It's OK. It really is OK. I just want to have a quiet, early night. I'll be fine in the morning."

And in the morning he did seem fine. We talked, played, and laughed as before.

But later, in my room, he told me of his terrible fear that I was the only person he would ever love. I was shocked, and even a little frightened by his intensity.

When the holidays were over and we went back to school he didn't reply at first to the letters I sent him. Then I received a note that read, 'It's easier if you don't write.'

I didn't tell anyone. What would I say? My brother misses me . . . too much. I missed him a great deal, but not too much. It was a question of degree, you see. Who can judge these matters? Certainly not a young girl.

I continued to write to him. He didn't reply. At

Easter he gave me my letters back unopened, and said, "Please, it's easier, it really is easier when you don't write. I miss you more and more. I cannot see how I can live a separate life. But I must. I have no hope of any other life, do I? You are changing. The boys at school talk all the time of girls—girls like you. One day, one of them will take you away from me. Completely away."

"But Aston, one day you and I will have boy-friends and girlfriends. We'll grow up and marry. We'll have our own children."

He looked at me, astounded.

"You have no idea what I'm talking about, have you? I want to be with you all the time. When I'm away from you I can only survive by blocking all thoughts of you from my mind. I work like a mad-man. You heard Papa about my report, I'm top of my year at virtually everything. I'm going to be top of my year for ever."

I didn't write to him at all the next term. In my last week he sent a little card which simply read, 'Thank You.'

That summer we seemed to be our old happy selves again. My mother sought in vain to arrange teenage parties. Children of friends came to stay. But Aston and I were only truly happy with each other. We were more like children than young ado-lescents. He dazzled me with his knowledge of mythological heroes and Greek gods. I impressed him with my skill at the piano.

When I started my new term in September I be-gan to write to him again.

He replied immediately.

'I think there is nothing in the world as terrible as Love. I need silence from you. I cannot bear it here otherwise. Aston.'

I didn't write again. When I talked to my mother on the phone, and asked about Aston, she said, "Everything's going to be all right. It's just adolescence, darling. I remember my own."

That Christmas, my body had almost settled into a shape that really hasn't changed much since. I felt very different from the summer before, heavier, stronger. I was developing much faster than Aston. He was taller. But his face, though thinner and more angular, still seemed basically unaltered.

His first words to me were, "Oh, Anna, Anna, how you have changed!"

He had tears in his eyes. He moved towards me slowly, awkwardly, as if he was wounded in some terrible way.

I began to feel ill-at-ease with him. Uncertain what behaviour was appropriate.

The first week seemed to pass in furtive glances, and nervous laughter, and dying conversations that never went anywhere.

My mother insisted on a Christmas party for 'the young people.' Aston protested violently at the idea.

"It's a cliché, parties with dancing. You can't force friendships. Leave us be."

But she was determined.

"You two are becoming positively reclusive. It's just not healthy. You need friends. This is a lovely time in your lives. Anna keeps turning down invitations to parties, it's ridiculous. As for you, Aston, you're so unfriendly to everyone, you don't get any. It's time it all stopped. I'm having a Christmas party here. That's that." The invitations went out to all the children of the right age that she knew in her circle. Not an enormous number, but enough.

Aston was impossible. He wouldn't dress properly. He was barely civil to the guests.

I had a marvellous pink dress, I remember. I found I enjoyed the dancing and all the flattery, the looks, and the fumbling of the more daring boys.

Aston kept leaving the party. He kept disappearing then reappearing with a haunted look on his face.

He came to my room when the party had ended. He was weeping. "I know everything is about to change forever. You are changing, Anna. We have had our last summer. I don't think I like the world very much anymore."

He came into my bed, and we lay chastely side by side.

But young boys in their early teens cannot lie chaste for long, beside a female body. Suddenly he was erect. Such a little movement, such a fleeting caress and his semen was on my stomach. He wept. His tears ran down my breasts. I felt as though I had received some strange benediction. Semen and tears. They would always be symbols of the night for me.

The next day we kept a distance from each other. It seemed better that way. I had a date that evening. One of the boys from the party had asked me to a dinner dance.

My vanity, and my new confidence, made me dress carefully, in a white dress with a low neckline. Aston opened the door for me, with a mock bow of both contempt and anger.

When I returned, I sat in the boy's car outside our house. Unexpectedly, he kissed me. Then he tried awkwardly to touch my breasts. I was not unduly alarmed. In fact, pleasure was my main emotion. As I turned to get out, I saw Aston. He was gazing down at us from an upstairs window. I have never forgotten the look on his face, and yet even after all these years I have not found the words to describe it. Perhaps there are human expressions which only the artist can catch.

He followed me into my bedroom.

"Next time he will go further," he said. "The time after that, even further. Until one night he will fuck you. That's the perfect description of what will happen to you."

"Oh, darling Aston, please, please don't." I was crying now. They seemed such terrible words, 'He will fuck you.' Aston looked almost ugly as he said them.

He left the room. I locked the door. I don't know why I did that. But it was very deliberate. I heard him shortly afterwards rattle the handle of the door. He whispered to me and the words were muffled as though he was sobbing:

"Anna, Anna, I'm so sorry, I'm so sorry, Anna. You've locked yourself away from me. I can't bear it. Oh, it will get worse. I know it. It will. It must get worse. I'm doomed. There's no hope for me."

I did not open the door. I lay there trying to calm

myself, to work out what was happening. Then I fell asleep.

I was awakened by a most awful sound. It was not a scream exactly. It was as though a desperate cry for help was being choked off, and then being released again. It was an animal sound. I fell out of bed and raced towards the door. My room was opposite Aston's and as if in a dream I saw my father trying to pull my mother from Aston's bathroom. My father was struggling so much with his burden as he tried to move towards the bedroom door that he seemed to be inching his way across Aston's room.

"Don't go in there, Anna! Don't move any further."

But I ran past him to the bathroom door. Aston was lying in the overflowing bath. His wrists were cut, and his neck was slashed and the blooded water splashed my feet. He looked like some pale doll creature, who was not dead, but who had never been alive. I pulled a little bathroom stool to the side of the bath and sat there cradling his head. My father came back with the doctor.

My father looked at us, and whispered, "Impossible, it's impossible that what I see is true. Impossible. Possible."

The doctor took my hands away from Aston's head. "Now, Anna, come with me. Come with me, come downstairs, there's a good girl. Sit with your mother. My wife is on her way, and Captain Darcy and your father's assistant will be here soon. I'm going to give you a sedative which will calm you."

Soon it seemed an army of people, quiet, competent, calm, were packing bags and moving through the house and night. It was as though they had learned some technique for dealing with terror. The technique was denial, discipline, and silence.

My mother and I were spirited from our house to that of my young friend. He stood shocked and frightened in the doorway. The girl, from whose white dress he had only hours before tried to prise the unfamiliar treasure of her breasts, now trembled before him, an old raincoat thrown over her bloody nightdress. Then the silent army took over again and guided us inside.

"Take Anna to Henrietta's room, Peter." Someone handed Peter a bag. My mother started to become hysterical again. All attention turned to her.

Peter led me upstairs and into Henrietta's room. The room was pink, with pink ruffles everywhere, and dolls dressed in pink were neatly arranged on the bed. A giant pink giraffe stood in a corner. A long mirror faced me. I walked towards the door, and turned the key in the lock. In the mirror, I watched my figure flit back across the room holding the boy's hand. I turned and faced him and heard my voice whisper, "Fuck me."

He was only eighteen at the time but with what care and kindness and love he did what I asked.

"I am now going to have a bath. Perhaps you would stand outside the door?" And he did. I bathed, slipping under the water again and again, knowing with glorious, triumphant certainty that I would live.

In Henrietta's baby-pink room I dressed in the jeans and shirt someone had packed for me, then I went down the stairs into my new life.

What is there to say of funerals? They are all the same and each one is unique. They are the ultimate separation, the ultimate letting go. For which of us would willingly join the body in its coffin in earth or fire or water? Life is usually loved more than our most sacred love. In that knowledge lies the beginning of our cruelty and of our survival.

Aston had loved me more than life itself. That was his destruction.

Over the years, these events followed. Some of them I've already told you. My parents divorced. I went to college in America. Then I came to England and became a journalist.

If all this has been presented to you in a flat voice, that's because the truth of a life can never be told. I send you a journalist's report. Some photographs would complete it.

My story has taken only a night to report to you. It has taken thirty-three years to live. The dailiness of it all fades away—others fade away. So few pages for Aston's life! In your life how many pages for me? The external tale of a man's life can be turned by any journalist into an article or two. And even after years of research by a biographer can only be extended to a book that can be read in two or three weeks.

And so here is my story, on a few pages. The map of my journey to you. Not to explain myself to you. That is unnecessary. But as one would show a photograph to one's beloved, and say, 'That's how I was then,' and smile at the lost creature of childhood. My 'photograph' elicits tears rather than smiles, but the creature is lost either way.

The dawn is coming. I'm tired. The type looks cold and dark on the white page . . .

Anna

It was delivered to my office the following morning. It was marked personal and confidential and thereby drew some furtive glances from my secretary.

Anna was right. It was a map. That was all. A gift I would treasure. I had known her the first moment I had seen her.

I went for a short walk, touching the letter in my pocket as I went over its contents in my mind.

Mean thoughts came to me. Perhaps her terrible tale was told in order to furnish her with an excuse for her suggested arrangement of marriage to Martyn and a life lived profoundly also with me.

She spoke of arrangements. Why didn't I examine some possible arrangements myself? Divorce Ingrid. Marry Anna. Martyn is young. He will get over it. And what of Ingrid? It had never been a passionate marriage and she had great reserves of strength. She had her large network of friends. She would survive. Sally too could cope well. After all, what I contemplated was a commonplace cruelty. The only unusual aspect was Martyn's relationship with Anna.

My career would be damaged, certainly. But it could weather the storm. I was not so ambitious that my career would count for very much, if I had to choose between a public life and a life with Anna.

But Anna had said she would not marry me. Oh, but

she will, she will, I told myself. Visions of Anna and me as man and wife—breakfasts together, dinners with friends, holidays together—flooded my mind. I felt sick. The visions had a hideous incongruity. It wouldn't work. We were made for other things. For needs that had to be answered day or night—sudden longings—a strange language of the body. An inner voice cried, 'Anna won't marry you.' And she was right. Her arrangement was pure. No one would suffer. The surface could remain exactly as it was. Ingrid and I, Sally, Martyn and Anna, each of us continuing along our chosen path.

After all, I had lived a life that had never been real to me. I could surely continue to give my performance, now that at last I had a real life. The one Anna had given me.

TWENTY-FOUR

"Anna's stepfather is in town for three days, at some writers' conference. Martyn suggested we have him to dinner. I must say I rather jumped at the idea. We agreed Thursday. I checked with your office. They said that would be OK."

"Good."

"Ever read any of his books?"

"Yes—two, actually."

"Oh, my intellectual husband."

"Hardly!" I lived in a country where reading two books by one of America's best-known modern writers classed me as an intellectual.

"Well, what's he like as a writer? He's very famous."

"He writes about alienation. Middle-class urban alienation. Twentieth-century America, divorced from its roots, with all its old values disappearing under the twin burdens of greed and fear."

"God! That doesn't sound too thrilling."

"To be fair, that's a rather clinical summary. He's a brilliant writer. His female characters are particularly well drawn. Even feminists like him."

"How long has he been married to Anna's mother?" asked Ingrid.

"I've no idea."

"What age is he?"

"He must be in his sixties. Mid-sixties, I'd have thought."

"Well, it might give me a different viewpoint on Anna. I'm really looking forward to Thursday. I'm going to attempt one of his books. Do you think they're in your study?"

"Possibly. I'll go and check." I found them easily. "Here they are," I said to Ingrid, who had followed me. "*The Glory Boy* and *Bartering Time*."

"Which is easier? No . . . which is shorter?"

"Try *The Glory Boy*."

"I won't finish it by Thursday, but I'll have some idea, won't I?"

"You will indeed, Ingrid. He's got a very specific style which permeates all his books. I must go. You look lovely in that beige dress. *Très chic*."

"*Merci, chéri—au revoir*."

Now that my real self lived and walked and breathed as Anna's creature, oh lucky creature, there were days when I enjoyed my role as Ingrid's husband more than I ever had before. I felt no guilt. All would be well with Ingrid. That morning I had an extraordinary illusion that she knew, and that she understood. She smiled so happily at me as I left, I was almost giddy with relief and joy.

TWENTY-FIVE

Wilbur Hunter had presence. Wilbur Hunter was aware that he had presence. I watched him gaze at Ingrid with solemnity mixed with intense interest.

As he accepted a whisky, he said: "You know, I haven't seen Anna for a long time. I've never even been invited to meet her friends before. So this is a very special occasion."

"How long is it since you last visited London?"

"Oh, five, six years."

"Has it changed?"

"I don't let it change. It's frozen in my heart as the place in which I met Anna's mother, twelve years ago. I refuse to see any changes either in London, or in her."

"How gallant," said Ingrid.

"Contrary to my image, I'm a romantic at heart. Are you a romantic?"

His query was clearly directed at me. I could see something strange in his gaze.

"Oh, yes," said Ingrid. "In a very subtle way, I think he's quite romantic."

"Anna's not a romantic. Are you, Anna?"

"No."

"Have you found that, Martyn? Or perhaps you disagree."

"As you said earlier, Wilbur, a romantic refuses to see changes in people he loves, or in cities which hold amorous memories for him. The meaning of 'romantic' could actually be 'untruthful.' Would you agree?"

"And Anna," said Wilbur, "is a very truthful girl."

"Yes," said Martyn. "She is totally truthful. I find that extraordinarily moving, and more exciting than romantic."

"Indeed," said Ingrid, feeling the conversation take on an edge she was unused to.

"It's a cliché, of course," said Wilbur, "but I find there are so many versions of truth. Versions of the truth may be perfectly acceptable, as most of the time nobody knows the whole truth, do they?"

"That sounds slightly cynical." I tried to lighten things a little. "Romance, like idealism, may be the last refuge of the cynic."

Martyn laughed. Wilbur turned to him.

"You haven't given yourself away, Martyn. Are you the cynic masked as romantic, the dissembler in the mask of truth?"

"I'm like Anna. I'm truthful. However, I am prepared to accept from others their own version of reality. I think it is a basic freedom really, to create one's own reality from whatever truths are available."

"I can see already that you and Anna are well suited. Anna tells me you are interested in writing novels, Martyn."

"Yes. But then quite a few journalists say that."

"But you mean it," said Anna.

Martyn looked embarrassed.

"You've never mentioned this to me, Martyn." There was a shaming note of petulance in my voice. I tried to change my tone. "I mean, that's very interesting."

"Well, Dad, it's my secret life." He laughed.

"I have no children," said Wilbur. "Maybe that's why I'm always examining them in my writing. And what obsesses you, Martyn? A writer is always obsessed by something."

"I'm obsessed by the subject we have just been discussing. Truth. I'm obsessed by the question of whether it exists as an absolute. Can a liar be giving the most accurate description of someone else's reality? That's why I love journalism. It's the perfect training for what I want to explore as a writer."

Martyn's voice continued, but I was unable to absorb his words. Stunned by admiration and jealousy, I realised that my son, cloaked in his own reality of beauty and intelligence, had become at last and most dangerously my rival.

"I hate to interrupt, but dinner's ready. Let's go in," said Ingrid.

She had received her long-agreed signal from Alice, 'our treasure' as Ingrid called her.

"You know, I'm truly glad to meet you all. It was a great delight to Anna's mother to hear of this invitation." Wilbur smiled at us all as he sat down.

"When did you last see your mother, Anna?" Ingrid looked at Anna.

"Almost two years ago."

"That's a very long time," said Ingrid quietly.

"All families are different." Martyn leapt to her defence.

"The mother-daughter relationship is particularly difficult, I think," said Wilbur.

"You write about it so sensitively in *The Glory Boy.*" Ingrid glanced at me triumphantly.

"Thank you, Ingrid."

"Anna sees her father more regularly. He lives in England."

Ingrid looked again at Anna.

"Yes, I do see Father more often. It's easier. I saw my mother regularly when I went to college in America. Wilbur has always been very kind."

"Who wouldn't be kind to you?" Martyn gazed lovingly at Anna. Suddenly he took her hand and kissed it.

A voice in my head drummed orders. Stay still, stay still. Say nothing. Do nothing. If you can't handle this, what in hell can you handle? The pain will go. It will go in a minute. This is nothing. This is pre-dinner banter.

I wanted to scream at him, 'Don't touch her! Don't touch her!'

Don't touch the hand of my slave! Slave! Come to me now! Here! In front of everyone! Let me worship you! Slave! Let me kneel to you!

Look at him. Look at him, the hated inner voice continued, think of all those women in his past. This is no young man in love with the magnetic stranger. He's her match, he's anybody's match. He's your match. He's your match round a dinner table, you arrogant fool. He's your match in bed. Face up to this now. Bed, bed, with Anna. When and how often? Think about it. Look at them now.

You can't take this. You can't handle this. You've never handled anything in your life. What on earth made you imagine you could stay sane in this situation? It's me or it's Martyn. I must, must have her. I can't breathe, I can't breathe.

"Darling! What is it? Your hand! You've crushed your glass in your hand! Martyn, run to the kitchen, get a cloth and the first-aid kit."

I looked at my bleeding hand and the crushed particles as they fell to the table.

"Oh, honestly, it's just a small cut. You see, Wilbur, the violence of the English family dinner."

Wilbur laughed. I felt deeply grateful to him. He had cleverly, perhaps deliberately, robbed the moment of its drama.

Ingrid was at her most impressive. Cool, in charge, expertly bandaging cut thumb and finger. The slivers of broken glass were spirited away by Alice. Suddenly a white napkin covered the red stain on the table. Like the sheet they throw over dead bodies.

"Continue. The foolish father has now recovered. All is well. Let's get back to reality. Or at least to Martyn's version of it."

Perhaps it was my tone, or the lull after the storm in the broken wine glass, but silence greeted me. I looked at Ingrid, who smiled wanly at me, and at Anna, who looked sad, then at Wilbur, who now looked embarrassed. Finally, I turned to Martyn. He looked back with concern and kindness. I felt a force that almost made me cry out, 'Martyn, my son, my son!' But of course no cry was heard, because no cry was made. Then the hostess rescue operation was under way again.

I applauded Ingrid silently. Well done, Ingrid. What a light touch you have. Lightness is all. Am I drunk? Surely not. Wine spilled is not the same as wine drunk.

We filed out of the dining room, and spread ourselves

in various parts of the sitting room. I sat as far away from everyone as possible. Wilbur sat close to Martyn. Anna, who had again revealed nothing of herself in public, sat quietly beside Ingrid on the sofa.

They were a study in opposites. Ingrid, her blond hair dressed and gleaming, wore a ruby-coloured silk shirt and a grey velvet skirt. Anna, short black wisps of hair seemingly painted on her forehead, wore a scoop-necked black wool dress.

"Ingrid . . . everyone . . . I'm so sorry. There's a late sitting at the House. I must go, it's nearly eleven."

"Can you drive? What about your hand?"

"Absolutely. It's nothing."

"And I must leave as well." Wilbur stood up.

"Darling, you can drop Wilbur, can't you?"

"No, no, I wouldn't hear of it," Wilbur interrupted.

"We'll take you later—have another coffee, Wilbur." Martyn spoke.

I stood undecided for a moment.

"Wilbur, come with me. It's on my way. You're at the Westbury, aren't you?"

"Yes."

We got into the car. I started driving.

"Anna's never done this before, you know," said Wilbur. "I think that maybe she's happy at last. Oh, we've met men occasionally, but never their families. Of course, Peter's mother and Elizabeth are very close."

"Peter?"

"Oh, I think it started as a young romance."

I remembered the boy in the pink bedroom on the night Aston died.

"They had a kind of on/off thing. It lasted for years,

but she couldn't settle with him. He wanted to marry, she didn't. They split up. He married pretty quickly after that—disastrously, I'm told. Do I assume from this dinner that Anna and Martyn are serious about each other?"

"Possibly."

There was an awkward silence. Then Wilbur spoke.

"You have a problem, my friend."

"In what way? What do you mean?"

"Men who crush wine glasses in their hands while devouring young women with their eyes suffer more than superficial wounds. Remain silent, my friend, remain silent."

Granite, and lights, and a turbulence of people flashed past. Too late for silence. Too late.

"Anna has brought a great deal of pain to a number of people. She is completely blameless, in my opinion. But she is a catalyst for disaster. Martyn may be different. He seems to let her be. That is vital with Anna. Try to hold her, and she will fight. You can't break Anna. She's already broken, you see. She must be free. That way, she will always return home. Of course, this is the advice I should be giving to the groom, and not to his father. But Martyn doesn't seem to need it. So you, my friend, should heed what I say. It's clearly too late for the only advice that could save you. Stay away from Anna."

"Your hotel, I think." I stopped the car.

"Thank you. I am as the grave, sir. I carry more secrets than you can imagine. We will almost certainly meet again. From my demeanour you will doubt we ever had this conversation. Good night, and good luck."

And he was gone.

I caught a glimpse of my face in the wing mirror. I

thought suddenly of my old, careful life. Was I paying the price of goodness? Of a well-lived life? Of goodness without feeling? Of love without passion? Of children not longed for? Of a career not craved for? Sin was the price. Sin. Did I, for once in my life, have the courage for sin?

My face in the mirror told me nothing. The face which had earlier told everything to Wilbur.

The vote over, I left the House at two thirty.

I drove past Anna's house. Martyn's car was not there.

I had to be in that room again. I needed to bring the painting back to life. I had to see limbs arranged as I remembered. I must gaze at her body on the table. I had to enter that world again. Immediately.

The darkness of the street, with its intermittent islands of light from the street lamps, and the sleeping mystery of the small, silent house, combined to give an edge to my desire. The edge of fear. Fear that she might not be there. Fear that she was with Martyn now, in the house. Fear twisted desire. I was almost gasping as I rang the bell.

Lights, footsteps, and she stood before me. I brushed past her into the hall.

I glanced upstairs. "Martyn is not here?"

"No."

"I gambled. There was no car." She was wearing a dark silk dressing gown. It had a masculine cut. As I followed her towards the room, an image of a boy with dark curly hair and strong back moving before me made me shudder. It was a memory of an adolescent Martyn, walking in a dark paisley dressing gown down the hall, as I returned from a late-night sitting of years ago.

She swung around, and the image died as the dressing gown fell open over her breasts. She led me to the table. I used the silken belt, and the black loose silk underneath, in a tableau of deliberate movements and restrictions, that at various times deprived my slave of vision and of speech. Unseen, I could worship her. Without the possibility of her spoken consent I could make the eternal demands of erotic obsession.

When it was over, I threw the dressing gown over the limbs I had so carefully arranged, as centuries ago painters covered the nakedness of the figures in the Sistine Chapel. Under the silk, her power hidden, she lay quietly watching me as I paced around the room. Terrible thoughts and fears again consumed me.

"Who is Peter?"

"I've told you about him before."

"I know. But update it, Anna. Update it for me."

"Why?"

"Because the truth of Peter as a boy who made love to you on the night Aston died, and the truth of Peter as someone you lived with and nearly married, are very different truths."

"But not relevant to the story I told you."

"Story?"

"The story I told you."

"That's all it is to you, a story?"

"How can it possibly be more? You didn't know me then, or Aston, or Peter. In that ignorance other people's lives are always only stories. The images I gave you were like illustrations. If I disappeared from your life tomorrow, that's all you would have. Images in a story, gestures frozen in a frame."

"Well, give me some new image of Peter."

"He limps. Badly. From a skiing accident he had a few months ago."

"How do you know?"

"Because I saw him, some time ago."

"I thought he was married now."

"Yes."

"Did you see him alone?"

"Yes."

"Where?"

"In Paris."

I left the room. I found the lavatory. I was sick. I washed my face, then, wrapping a towel around my waist, I walked slowly back to Anna.

She had left the table. She sat smoking a cigarette in a chair by the window. The dark green velvet of the curtains blended with what I now saw was an olive silk gown. Her face, and the waves of her black hair, seemed almost a Renaissance cameo, spoiled by the incongruity of the cigarette.

"About Paris. Tell me."

"Martyn and I checked out of L'Hôtel. After lunch I visited Peter. Martyn went shopping. We met up later."

So as I lay in a drunken haze in L'Hôtel trying to reach out and catch her presence in the room she had deserted, she had been with Peter.

"Where did you see him?"

"In his apartment."

"What about his wife?"

"She was in New York. They are virtually separated."

"How did you know she was in New York?"

"I rang him."

"Before you went to Paris?"

"Yes."

"So Martyn went to Paris with you, believing he was going to have a weekend with his lover. I am accurate in that, am I not?"

"Yes."

"And I went to Paris because I could not survive the day without seeing you. And you, Anna, you went to Paris to see Peter."

"No. That's not quite true. I wanted to go to Paris with Martyn. You followed me. You needed me. I came to you."

"And Peter?"

"Peter is always there, in the background."

"A lurking presence in the corner."

"If you want."

"Why does it take virtually an inquisition to get even a glimmer of the truth from you?"

"Because I find people ask questions when they are ready for the answers. Before that, they usually guess, or sense, the truth. But they don't know for certain. When they want to know, they ask. It's dangerous either way."

"Dangerous. Why?"

"Because I hate being questioned. On the other hand, I try not to lie. Tonight you came for me. I was there, I will always, somehow, be there. What else matters? If I answered every question you wanted to ask—what would you gain? We have our story. Leave it alone. Leave everybody else in my life alone. As I do with you. I never ask you about Ingrid. Or about other women—have there been others?"

I shook my head.

"We know this is extraordinary. We knew it the second we met. It will never happen again in our lives. Let it be."

"I can't watch you with Martyn. I just can't. It's impossible. I can block it off when I don't see you together. But tonight . . . watching you both, I felt such violence. I felt I could harm Martyn."

"But instead you crushed a glass. Don't worry, you won't commit any act of violence. Physically you will control yourself."

"How do you know that?"

"Because of us. You are at the extremes of yourself with me. There is no further to go. Try not to see me with Martyn. Stay away, make an excuse."

I threw myself on my knees in front of her.

"Anna, leave Martyn. Just finish it. I will leave Ingrid. In time we can be together publicly, and until then discreetly."

She jumped up, and moved away from me.

"Never, never. I will never do that."

"Why? My God, why not?"

"Because I don't want more from you than I already have. And what we already have would be destroyed by you, if we were together."

"No. No, you're wrong."

"I can see from your face that you know I'm right. You would be full of doubts and fears. And you would have reason, sometimes. I will, for example, always see Peter. Maybe I would want to see Martyn. I will not change the way I live my life. I have promises to keep. Debts to pay to people. I will not be forced to change that."

"But I'd give you that freedom. I would. I'd teach myself."

"You couldn't. You would be in a deeper hell than you can possibly imagine. All the agony, the pain for Ingrid, for Martyn, your guilt, and for what? For nothing more than you have now, or need. And in time you would jeopardize even that."

"Has Martyn asked you to marry him?"

"No. Not yet."

"But you think he will?"

"Yes."

"Why will you marry him?"

"Because Martyn asks no questions. Martyn lets me be."

"Is that the extent of your demands on people? That they just let you be?"

"It's a very heavy demand. So far, Martyn is the only person who has been able to meet it."

"Well, clearly I can't."

I took my clothes, and I dressed in silence. She lit another cigarette and began to speak.

"What exists between us exists in one dimension only. To try to trap this in an ordinary life will destroy us both. You will never lose me. As long as I live. You will never lose me."

"And Martyn?"

"Martyn will never know. It's up to us both to ensure he never knows. Some things about me, Martyn guesses. But our pact, our way of handling each other, grows stronger all the time. All will be well."

"If you and Martyn married, where could we meet?"

"What a practical question for a night like this." She turned her face to me so that in the half light it seemed to float in a sea of dark green, the green of the curtain and her collar of gleaming olive.

She looked so sure, so strong. Like some goddess to whom one could safely hand one's destiny, certain that her decisions would be right, her judgement wise. We were colluding in a life plan of betrayal and deceit that involved the breaking of age-old taboos, as well as the more ordinary cruelty of adultery. And we knew that we would continue to the end. We were designing our world, and those most closely bound to us, into a semblance of order. An order which would allow us our essential, blazing, structured chaos of desire.

"I will buy a small flat. We will meet there. Leave all of this to me. It is easier for me. Now you must go." She smiled as we parted at the door. "Let everything . . . just be."

It was nearly dawn when I climbed into bed beside Ingrid. "So sorry," I whispered. "John Thurler captured me—he went on and on, you know how he does."

She groaned in sympathy, and half opened her eyes for a second. Then her breathing resumed its steady rhythm. I lay there in the darkness, wondering how I could breathe at all.

TWENTY-SIX

"I've received a letter from Martyn thanking me very charmingly for the trust fund I helped set up. You know its terms. Does this mean wedding bells?" Edward was on the phone.

"Possibly."

"What a pity Tom died before Martyn became a young man. He would have been very proud of him. I miss Tom, you know. Marvellous man, marvellous character."

"I know." The mention of my father suddenly conjured up my days as the son I had long forgotten. The days when I was my father's son, as well as my son's father.

"I've been very lucky," said Edward. "I've seen Ingrid happily married for all these years. Now there's the possibility of Martyn getting married. Not sure about Anna. Clearly Martyn loves her . . . so I'm going to warm towards her. Sally and Jonathan seem very jolly together. You could find yourself with both of them married soon—how about that?"

I tried to sound relaxed and pleased. I even gave an imitation of an Edward-style chortle.

"How are things with that Committee you're chairing?"

"So-so."

"Soul of discretion, aren't you? Mark my words, you'll be promoted at the next reshuffle. You're a bit of a dark horse, even to me! But it works, your semi low profile. People do like you. They trust you. Trust is a minor miracle these days. No one seems to trust anyone anymore. Ah well, if this does end in an engagement between Martyn and Anna, I'd like the wedding to be held at Hartley. What do you think? I know it's normally the girl's family's place. But her parents are divorced. Her mother lives in America. I'm probably jumping the gun, it's just an idea. Say something."

"It's a very nice idea, Edward. But they're not even engaged yet."

"Quite, quite so. Engagement party then, at Hartley." He laughed. "I never give up, do I? It's age, you know. I'm clinging more and more tenaciously to my family. I don't want to let go. Very odd, old age. Always knew it would happen, if I was lucky. I just didn't expect it so soon. You see . . . it comes too soon. Must let you go. Tom and I did well, I think, for Martyn and Sally. Ingrid will get Hartley, obviously. Plus quite a lot . . . well . . ."

"Edward. Please. You've been marvellous to us and to the children. We've all got years together. Years ahead of us."

"I hope so. Sorry if this all got a bit sentimental. It's the idea of Martyn marrying. Couldn't say it earlier, but of course it brings back the loss of Ingrid's mother. Terrible sadness still, you know. Now this time I'm finishing. Take care."

"You, too. Bye, Edward."

I put the phone down, and with some determination tried to blind myself to a vision of my father.

You may not be a son anymore, he seemed to say, but my God you have one.

What are you doing? What kind of father are you?

You were always a distant son. Always distant from your mother and me. And a cold son becomes a cold father.

Maybe I had a cold father.

I saw the vision of his face turn away from me. I dreamed I saw all his years of failed love crush him.

TWENTY-SEVEN

We were in the bedroom. I never really thought of it as ours. Certainly I never thought of it as mine. It was the bedroom where Ingrid and I spent that time of our marriage—the room which tells the real story of a man and woman in that strange arrangement. But the story has no observers other than the participants. They must in most cases lie to themselves, and to each other. The secrets of the bedroom lie buried under layers of time and custom, children, work, dinner parties, illnesses, and the myriad other rituals and events with which we dull the pain.

Ingrid was at the dressing table applying a layer of cream to her face and neck. She took great care not to touch the satin straps that lay on her pale, delicate shoulders.

'Blondes have dry skin' is one of life's absolutes emblazoned on my mind. Though she was never in any way a frivolous woman, her morning and evening ritual was vital to Ingrid. I had never known her to miss it. The familiar sight of patting was regularly accompanied by the repetition of the essential truth, 'I know it's a bore. But blondes do have dry skin.'

"Wilbur rang to thank us for dinner. He's quite fascinating, I think. Don't you?" Ingrid spoke.

"He writes better than he talks."

"Oh, really? I thought he was very interesting at dinner."

"I don't know. I found it all rather banal actually, the glories of truth, et cetera."

"He likes Martyn a great deal. Do you think Martyn will become a writer? It seems quite extraordinary to me that he never mentioned it before. I mean, it's not as if we've ever put any pressure on him one way or the other. I'm quite pleased really."

"He might just have said it to impress Wilbur."

"Oh, no. Martyn's not bothered about impressing anyone. Except Anna, perhaps. Wilbur says her mother will be very pleased to hear that Anna looks so well and happy. They're not close, as we gathered. How lucky we are with our children. Frankly, our doubts about Anna— the age gap and so on—are really trivial in a way. I mean, so what, she's older and a bit more sophisticated. He could have fallen in love with someone much more unsuitable. What do you think?"

"Yes. I think we've been blessed."

"Anyway, I've made up my mind to put my worries to one side and get to know her a bit better. Up to now, I've been a bit cool, don't you think?"

"You've always been very nice."

"Yes, I know that. But 'very nice,' it's not the same as really friendly, is it? Mind you, can one ever be really friendly with one's son's wife?"

"They're not married yet, you know. They're not even engaged."

"Yes. But you know what I mean. It's different for men. They don't feel the same sense of loss when a son marries. Maybe you feel a little jealous of Sally's boyfriend, Jonathan?"

"I never give him a thought."

"Hmm! That's slightly your problem. You give the impression sometimes that you don't really think very much about the children . . . their future . . . their relationships."

"Don't be silly."

"That remark about Sally's boyfriend is just typical. If I didn't keep on about Anna you'd probably never give her a thought either."

My back was to her. I closed my eyes. A sudden shame at the meanness of the deceit, and the cruelty of the evasion, came over me. I could neither move nor answer.

"Darling? Darling, are you all right?"

I spun round, and realised that Ingrid had seen my back in the mirror. Perhaps some line of my shoulder or body had told its own story. Certainly the face I saw in the mirror as I turned to her was that of a man in deep distress.

Ingrid's eyes filled with love as she approached me. Her nearness, and my guilt, led to a rage within me. Ugly and menacing, my reflection stared back at me.

"What's the matter? What's the matter?" she cried.

"Nothing. Nothing. Age, I suppose. I suddenly felt old."

"Oh, darling! Darling, it's because the children are on the verge of marriage, that's all. You're not old. You're still the most attractive man I know."

She was close to me. Her body, satin-contoured, rested against mine in a familiar embrace. I put my hands on her shoulders, and keeping a chasm of inches between us, kissed her forehead. Then I moved away. It was a rejection. We both knew it.

"Is there something you haven't told me?" She was not looking at me as she creamed her hands.

"Of course not."

"Are you worried about something? The Committee perhaps . . ."

"No! Nothing. Ingrid, I'm sorry. I just suddenly felt old and tired. It's passed now. I'm going downstairs to read a bit. I've got some papers I must work on. I'll come up later."

A look of anger flashed between us. I ignored it, and left the room.

Downstairs I poured myself a whisky. I must find a way of moving us quickly towards the marriage for which we were destined. A marriage of diminishing physical contact, which would cause neither comment nor heartbreak. Ours had never been a passionate marriage. Surely it must be possible to accelerate the already well-established route towards celibacy.

I must make it happen. Ingrid's physical closeness was becoming impossible for me to handle. A sickness for Anna wrenched my being. It was as though Ingrid had been trying to invade the space which the ghost of the absent Anna filled. The battle-charged air had made me ill.

You will make yourself very sick, an inner voice admonished. You know that. Don't you? Yes, doctor. Physician, heal thyself! I smiled wryly as I remembered the old adage. Perhaps punishment was what I needed?

Having made up my mind to a further sacrifice of Ingrid's happiness, I went to work on my papers.

Breakfast the next morning was monosyllabic and cool. To my shame, Ingrid's concern for me constantly triumphed over her desire to punish me.

I remained cool. I was anxious to keep a distance between us that would allow a new workable pattern to emerge. A finely judged thing, this careful undermining of the foundations of a marriage.

"I want to organise the birthday party for Father on the twentieth. I thought it might be nice if we could all arrive for dinner and stay for lunch on the Sunday. I'll talk to Ceci. I can plan the lunch menu now. Sally and I can help Ceci prepare everything. Then there's Anna, of course, she can help too."

This domestication of Anna seemed to me part of a plot on Ingrid's part. Did she not see the incongruity of Anna in a kitchen? I had a vision of the four women. Ceci, Ingrid, Sally, all busy and competent and on home territory, and Anna, weaving her mystery and her power round the kitchen. Anna, imbuing all with another female aura, one that was infinitely more potent than the charm of care and kindness. The others were cardboard cutout figures, and Anna alone was real, and glorious, and dangerous.

"I may be late down. I'll check, but Sunday lunch should be fine."

"Good. I'm sure Father will be thrilled. We can discuss presents later."

She looked at her watch. Ingrid was anxious to be the one who dismissed the other. A revenge for last night.

"I must be off," she said. I moved towards her to give the customary kiss on the cheek. But she just smiled briefly and as she turned her head slightly, my lips brushed her hair. Perhaps that was another subtle change in the ritual, to move from skin to hair on the ever-lengthening road away from each other's bodies.

In the car I remembered that it had been at Hartley I had asked Edward for permission to propose to Ingrid. So long ago. A fateful yes, that had led to Martyn and Sally, and to year upon year of peace and contentment, good luck and prosperity.

Hartley too would fall to Anna. Its other associations would be altered forever. Its walls and gardens, innocent of her till now, Ingrid's most beloved domain, must surrender too.

I rang her. It was early, she was home.

"Hartley!"

"Yes, I know. It was impossible to say no." Anna paused. "I don't think I mentioned it, but I'm going to be away next week, until Thursday evening."

I paused. Don't ask where. Don't push, I admonished myself.

She laughed as if she had read my thoughts and said, "I've got to go to Edinburgh for a feature I'm writing, that's all."

"Good. My Committee is at the proposal stage. Final documents need to be prepared."

"Life, it seems, goes on."

"The surface needs attention, I agree."

"The outer edges of our world need strengthening. Only then can our secret real life continue."

"We know each other very well."

"Indeed we do."

"Goodbye. Till Hartley."

"Till Hartley—goodbye."

TWENTY-EIGHT

Hartley had never held me in its thrall. It was Edward's home. The place where Ingrid had been born, and had spent her childhood. The place where she rode and fished with Edward in school holidays. 'Look, over there, I fell off Border. Father thought I had been killed. I was only concussed. There, that's where I used to sit and dream of my future. That's where, behind that rose bush, my first boyfriend kissed me!' I had listened to all her dreaming memories, with a politeness that should have worried me. A man in love does not listen to the tales of his beloved's childhood with such detachment. Nor does he look on the house that sheltered her with so cool an eye.

As I drove towards Hartley on Saturday evening I envisaged it as Anna would, seeing it for the first time.

Through iron gates, a long straight drive leads to its grey stone Gothic frontage. The massive oak door, around and above which Edward has grown ivy, has a reassuring solidity about it. Once one is inside and with the door closed, the panelled walls and high latticed windows impose their own quiet rhythm. The great carved oak staircase seems powerfully to separate the night from the day, so that each more fully enjoys its own charm.

The drawing room faces south over a formal lawn. Beyond that, Edward's land stretched out to soothe him with his mastery of all the eye could see.

The dining room, with its mahogany sideboard laden with silver, makes the deeply English statement 'Food may be serious, but it is not important.' Though sensible and tasty, meals are not the highlight of a weekend at Hartley. The heavy, unwelcoming dining room would defeat any culinary ambition.

The library is packed with books which would embarrass an educated European. Books on hunting, country walks, some biography—usually of military heroes—a little history. No classics, no poetry, no novels. Its easy chairs invite occupation, and are placed carefully beside tables laden with country magazines, the real reading matter of the house.

The only room downstairs in which I ever felt relaxed is the drawing room. I have virtually never visited the kitchen. Ceci, the cook, ruled supreme in her domain.

The staircase leads to a large landing and two corridors. One corridor leads past four suites down towards the large door to Edward's room.

A shorter, panelled corridor leads past two other bedroom suites towards a heavy oak door and the room which over the years has been designated to Ingrid and me.

The bedrooms, all panelled and sometimes entered by two or three little steps, are genuinely charming. Each has a different eiderdown in a flower pattern with matching cushions. They were all long ago embroidered by Ingrid's mother.

Over time, the rooms have taken on the names of the

flower or plant embroidered on the quilt—rose, or iris, or daffodil.

I knew this house so well and its rooms and its gardens, yet Hartley had not entered my soul. I visited Hartley, and after nearly thirty years I remained a visitor. Would Anna be as impervious to its charms?

I stopped the car. My reverie was ended. Ingrid, Sally, and Jonathan came to greet me in the drive. "Edward's on the phone in his room. Good journey?"

"Mm. Very quick."

"Anna and Martyn will be here later. Anna had some work to finish. I asked Ceci to delay dinner until nine fifteen. Hopefully, they will have arrived by then."

"Hello, sir."

I nodded towards Jonathan, and decided against first-name terms for a while.

Ingrid linked her arm in mine as we followed Sally and Jonathan into the hall.

"Edward put all the young people into his corridor, away from parents. We've got empty rooms the whole length of ours. Quite clever, don't you think?"

"Very."

"Come up and change."

Our room was called Rose. The quilt, patterned in red, white, and pink, was a potent reminder of lost days, and had an accusatory innocence as I entered.

Edward was in the drawing room when I came down.

"This is really wonderful of you all," he said. "Can't tell you how much I appreciate it. Birthdays don't mean so much now. Still, I suppose seventy-four is worth noting."

"Indeed it is." He looked well. He'd always had a glow about him, a kind of rosy hue. It suited him in old age.

"Have a drink?"

"Thanks, whisky please."

"Ingrid tells me Anna and Martyn will be along later."

"Yes."

"Nice of her to come. Must be a bit boring really. And Sally's chap, I'm rather touched they should make the effort."

"Nonsense, Edward. You're a favourite with all ages."

"Am I? Always wanted to keep in touch with young people. Gives one a feeling of continuity. Marvellous to have great-grandchildren. Any chance, do you think, before I pop off?"

"Edward, I wish you great-great-grandchildren."

"Aha—always the diplomat."

Ingrid came to the door. "They're here. I'll tell Ceci. They can have a quick bath and change, and then dinner. Perfect timing."

Anna wore trousers. They were grey and tailored. This informal, country look altered her in some way.

Greetings over, she went upstairs. Later she returned in a dark blue dress that I'd seen before. She still seemed different. She's ill-at-ease, tense, I thought. I'd never seen Anna ill-at-ease before.

Dinner was a quiet affair. Everyone was tired after their journey. It was a time for remembrances.

"Anna, what memories do you have of home?"

"Very few really. We travelled so much."

"I can't remember a life without Hartley," said Ingrid.

"Anna has her memories," said Martyn quickly. "But they're more varied—impressionistic almost. Sally's and mine are of Hartley, and of Hampstead."

"Was it difficult when you were young? Always moving," asked Sally.

"It was just very different, as Martyn said. My childhood is really only a series of impressions—of countries, towns, schools."

"And of meetings and partings." Martyn shot a smile of sympathy at Anna, an 'I understand, you're not alone anymore' kind of smile.

I gazed at the silver on the sideboard, and longed for dinner to be over. I could have avoided all this, I thought. I could have made excuses—good ones. But I wanted to be here. I had to be here.

"Martyn and I have been so lucky," said Sally. "A secure life in London. Lots of holidays at Hartley."

"The same little village in Italy every summer," said Martyn. "Repetition of rituals can be a kind of balm to the soul. I agree with Sally. We had idyllic childhoods . . . in lots of ways . . ."

"Not in every way?" Ingrid laughed.

"Oh, every ungrateful child has a list of ways in which their parents failed them. Mine's pretty short."

"Come on," said Edward, "you've got us all fascinated. What's on the list? Did they secretly beat you?" Edward rubbed his hands in glee.

"There was too much order . . . a lack of chaos and passion." Martyn's face became very still, as though he were mouthing the words. His voice was flat. It is thus we most often reveal inner pain. The effort of containment robs our words of colour and expression.

We looked at each other from either side of the table. A father who had missed knowing his son. A son who thought he knew his father.

"Well," said Jonathan, "if you want chaos and passion you should have lived in our house. My father was a perfect gentleman. But it's no secret he was a constant womaniser. He and my mother had the most terrible rows. Still, she stayed with him. For me and my sister, I suppose. They're very happy now. But then he's been ill for some time. It sounds cruel to say so, but she likes his weakness. He's rather surrendered to her, like a good child with a kind nurse."

"How time works on all the young men. The wild young men," sighed Edward. "The tales I could tell you!"

"Before you, Anna, Martyn was quite a young man about town," said Sally.

Anna smiled. "So I've heard."

"Oh! From whom?"

"From Martyn."

"Aha. A full confession, was it, Martyn?"

"Not at all," said Anna. "I was not surprised. Martyn is very attractive."

"He's extraordinarily good looking," said Ingrid. "And there speaks a proud Mum. Now let's all have a lovely early night. Somebody's got a birthday tomorrow." Ingrid kissed Edward.

On the landing the 'goodnight-and-sleep-well' wishes were a trifle embarrassed. Anna was at the end of Edward's corridor in Hyacinth. Martyn was beside her in Ivy.

"I used to think all this was too pretty and feminine. Then Edward explained how carefully and lovingly each bedspread and its matching cushions had been embroidered. Now I think of it as a lovely tribute to Grandma."

Ingrid stroked his cheek. "How kind you are, Martyn. Right, off we go. We're down here at the end of the corridor." She smiled at them all. It was a conspiratorial 'It's up to you, but don't embarrass anyone' smile.

We turned and walked to our bedroom. I felt a humiliation I had not felt before. My body seemed heavy and awkward. I leaned against the door as we closed it behind us.

"That was all a bit coy," I said sharply to Ingrid.

"Coy! Coy, what a strange word to use. We are another generation. It's quite understandable that they should want some certainty that we were not close to them. On the other hand, I don't want Edward embarrassed, hence the separate rooms. Anyway, I don't know how far things have gone with Jonathan and Sally. It saves tension all round. Anna and Martyn are different."

"You seem to be taking a great shine to Anna lately."

"Force majeure, darling." Ingrid started to undress. During the dressing table ritual with the creams she suddenly stopped, and said, "Something is happening between us. I don't understand it. But please don't think I am unaware of it. I know you've been faithful to me, I know you're not having an affair now. We've never been people for heart-to-heart conversations, so I'll just wait. Does it sound arrogant? About the affairs, I mean. I don't mean it to. Your faithfulness is very important to me. I just couldn't be a Jane Robinson. What Martyn said about the lack of chaos and passion . . . well, it's what I find attractive about you. And I still do. It all works in a way that's right for us, mostly. Doesn't it?"

"Oh, Ingrid. My dear, I'm so sorry. I know it's a terrible cliché, but I've got a problem and I must work it out myself. You're so wise to just let me sort it out in my own time."

We met each other's gaze. We managed to avert our

eyes before truth could be seen by either of us. Elliptical intimacy is the marriage vow of good companions. Vows that they honour behind the closed doors of bedrooms where, trapped in the winding sheets of dead desire, they take the pleasure they are entitled to. They convince themselves that they have not been cheated in this roulette game of passionless passion. It is a legacy from one generation to the next. The good marriage tie.

I lay beside Ingrid as she fell asleep. Anger and hatred worked in me, like snakes hissing. Their tongues were saying, Go and get her. Go get her. Just take her away, they whispered. Make her come with you. Make her leave Martyn. Tonight. Just give up everything. Now.

I wanted to twist, and turn, and wrestle with their obscenities. But I lay silent and quiet beside my sleeping beautiful wife.

At two o'clock I couldn't bear it anymore. I got up. As I opened the door I saw Anna standing outside one of the empty rooms in our corridor. It was Olive. She beckoned me and smiled a little. As we entered the room she said, "I chose this room for peace. I wondered whether you would come. I could see your pain."

I moved against her, desperate. She held her hand to her stomach and said, "No. I'm bleeding." Then she knelt down before me, lips parted, mouth open, waiting. I worshiped her. Her head was thrown back, her eyes were closed, as though in some ritual act of genuflection.

Subsumed into her. Consummation. Of a kind. Then, eyes open, I stared at the slight mutilation of her features which the forcing of her mouth had caused. Drained by her, I thought of the hopelessness of pleasure. I was still trapped within my own body.

The room was lit by moonlight. As she left me, she

said, "I said yes, today, to Martyn. He is going to tell the family tomorrow at lunch. He wants to make it a family celebration. It will be very hard for you. But please remember I am everything you need me to be. You live in me." She stroked her hand across her mouth and said, "Remember—everything, always." Then she slipped out the door.

I bowed my head in the darkened room. I felt as though a heavy weight had been placed across my shoulders. In the gloom the olive-embroidered spread and cushions filled my eyes. Conscious of their peace and beauty I lay down upon them. They were a grove of green in the moonlight. I felt the anger and hatred leave me. I could carry my burden. I could handle 'everything, always.'

After some time, I do not know how long, I slipped back into bed beside Ingrid and slept deeply. In the morning I knew I did not want to see Anna and I needed time before I could face Martyn. A new life was beginning. A life in which Anna and Martyn would be formally a couple. I must learn to carry the weight of this reality.

The tightness between my shoulder blades told me that it was a cross I had decided to bear. Others hide their pain in their bloodstream, or intestines, or it reaches the surface of their skin, daily stigmata. A childhood image from my Catholic nanny, one of her holy pictures of the cross being carried on the road to Golgotha, had all these years later become my body's image for my soul's pain.

"I'm going to have a quick tea and toast in the kitchen, then have a walk. I'll work up here until lunchtime. Do you mind?"

"Of course not. Everyone will understand," said Ingrid.

"It's just that at Hartley, breakfasts can go on till lunch."

Ceci was in the kitchen. She watched disapprovingly as I consumed the toast and tea standing by the table. Then, hearing Sally's laughter from the dining room, I opened the kitchen door and was gone.

I walked through the walled kitchen garden. Its ordered perfection reminded me that wild nature can be tamed and made to work for us. I walked into the meadow, where, in other days, ponies belonging to Ingrid, and then our own children, had grazed. Everything I saw, garden, meadows, the almost dry small stream, spoke of a life from which I was forever parted.

Who was the young man who had walked through this very meadow when courting Ingrid? Where was the father who had photographed Sally and Martyn as they trotted with awkward pride on their ponies?

I managed to return to my room without having to say good morning to anyone. I worked on my papers and tried to compose myself before lunch.

"To Edward." The toast was mine. "Happy Birthday and many happy returns from us all."

"To Edward." We all raised our glasses. Anna glanced nervously at Martyn. He rose to speak.

"Grandad . . . everyone . . . I've got something to tell you all. Anna and I thought it would be nice, in honour of your birthday . . . to announce our engagement! Mum . . . Dad . . ." He looked at us, eager, pleading, handsome. There was also a subtle look of triumph in his eyes.

"Well, well," said Ingrid, ". . . how marvellous. Congratulations, Martyn. Anna, I'm so happy for you both."

"Martyn, I can't tell you what this means to me," said Edward. "On my birthday too. So touching, boy, so touching." He looked at Ingrid. "Martyn always was a touching soul. You've done well, my dear," he said to Anna. "Don't mind me saying that, do you? He's very special, this grandson of mine. Mind you . . . he's very lucky too. Fine girl . . . thought so the second I met you."

Sally had jumped up and thrown her arms round her brother.

"Congrats, you two. It's great news."

Jonathan broke in with "Well done, Martyn! Mind you, I could see it coming a mile off. Couldn't I, Sally? I always said Anna and Martyn were made for each other. Right from the start. That super cool image you two have, it never fooled me for a minute. Head over heels in love. No doubt about it."

Say something now. You're the only one who hasn't spoken. Say something now. My mind raced.

"Martyn."

"Dad."

"What can a father say on such an occasion? It's a strange and wonderful day. My best wishes to you both."

It must have been all right because he smiled a 'Thanks, Dad' back at me.

"You'll get married from Hartley? You must . . ."

"Father! They've only just announced their engagement. Anna's parents may have their own ideas. It's the bride's parents . . ."

"Oh yes, I know all that. But with Anna's mother living in America, I just thought . . ."

"We can have great fun planning all this," said Ingrid.

"When are you thinking of actually getting married? Got a date fixed?"

"Not really," said Anna.

"As soon as possible," said Martyn. "We thought three months from now, if that's OK."

"Three months! It's not long." Ingrid was already planning the wedding.

"Actually we are probably just going to have a quiet wedding somewhere. Anna hates big weddings."

"Really," said Ingrid, trying to hide the disappointment in her voice.

"We felt a quiet wedding with family . . ."

"Family! Good heavens. You must let your parents know," said Ingrid. "And we must meet them soon."

"I'll ring them if I may." Anna looked at Edward.

"Of course, of course."

"I was going to do the traditional thing. You know, ask permission and all that. But Anna felt it was unnecessary. So here we are, Grandpa, interrupting your birthday."

"Yes, indeed you are," said a mock-angry Edward. "And I haven't even opened my presents. Let's all finish pudding and have champagne and presents in the drawing room. Then the happy couple can use my study for their phone calls."

As Anna passed me her eyes caught mine. I was pleased to see that she looked sad.

I drank my whisky, and watched the champagne add further to the gaiety as the party continued. Whisky is a strengthening drink. No man ever drank champagne in the midst of a defeat. After this defeat, there is no escape for you, I told myself. There was no anger or hatred either. Just an acceptance, a resignation to pain. I trusted Anna. She trusted me. If we wanted 'everything, always,' this was the best way. Her way.

To observe the joy of others, while in pain oneself, is to witness what looks like insanity overtaking ordinary people. All my years as the calm outsider didn't prepare me for the savage loneliness I felt that day. Clinging to the hope of Anna, I had to watch her move further and further away. Unable to call out to her, 'Help me, help me, I can't do this,' I tried to appear jovial. I accepted Edward's thanks for our gift—Ingrid had arranged an aerial photo of Hartley—and listened to the rise and fall of questions and answers about the future wedding of my son. Trapped, I knew I must show no fear. If I failed I would bring about the very thing that most terrified me—the total loss of Anna. The pain between my shoulder blades knotted its way deeper into me. The whisky seemed to sharpen my perception of all I saw. I longed for it to blur the edges.

Martyn and Anna went to Edward's study to phone her parents. A few minutes later Martyn came back.

"Mum, I think it would be nice if you would speak to Anna's mother as well. You're so good at these things. Wilbur asked to be remembered to you, Dad. Do you think we could have a word, Dad?"

"Mm. Of course."

Self-consciously, my son and I walked through the kitchen garden towards the meadow.

"It's strange to think of all those summers at Hartley. All before Anna," he said. "I find it hard to think of my life before her. Yet she's only been with me for such a short time. I suppose everyone feels that when they fall in love?"

"I expect they do."

"I know you and Mum had your doubts. Especially Mum. Oh, she never really said anything, but I could feel it. I understood it too."

"Did you?"

"Yes. Anna's a bit older. Not the kind of girl I brought home before." He laughed.

"Well, you certainly brought home, as you put it, quite a number."

"Were you shocked?"

"No. Not at all."

"You were always so proper. Oh, without being pious in any way" (he hurried this), "but you know they were all . . . fantastic."

"They were all very attractive. And blonde, as your mother pointed out."

"Yes. I went through rather a thing with blondes. This is an odd conversation to have with one's father, but I feel closer to you today than ever before. I felt like a prince during those years. It wasn't promiscuity. It was a kind of mad wildness."

"Which stopped with Anna."

"Yes, Anna is my life, Dad. I suppose I'm in thrall to her. It's an extraordinarily powerful thing. It's been so hard for me to be careful. To play it right, not to lose her. She's very complicated. She didn't think I could handle it in the beginning. Now she's confident."

"And from what do these complications arise?"

"Well, she had a difficult relationship with her brother. He's dead now. Then there was her parents' divorce. And she had a long relationship with a chap that didn't quite work either."

"What happened to her brother?" An evil father asked

the question. A good son replied, "Some ghastly tragedy. She doesn't talk about it much."

"And who was the chap she had this long relationship with?"

"His name was Peter. They nearly married, I think. Then she had a few other short-term things . . . you know . . ."

"Well, I would expect that. She's thirty-two, thirty-three, isn't she?"

"Mm. She's very sensitive. She hates being tied down. I had to be very careful. I had to give her lots of freedom yet still hold on." He paused self-consciously. "We've never talked like this before, have we?"

"No."

"I suppose getting engaged, particularly to someone like Anna, makes me feel . . . mature? Does that sound pompous?" He smiled at me. His handsomeness, his height, and his happiness all combined to make him seem like a young god striding towards his golden future. I felt like a heavy, weary attendant, doomed to watch the sun shine ever more brightly on this chosen child.

Martyn touched my shoulder.

"I wanted to say I'm sorry. What I said last night about chaos and passion was nonsense. You've been a marvellous father. A bit distant, but that's because of your work, and all the demands on you. Anyway, you've never let me down. And if we'd been very close and you'd seemed terribly involved, I'd probably have hated it. I also want to thank you for the trust. I'm sure you advised when the grandparents set it up. It's a great help. Anna and I are going to start house-hunting next week. Anna's got money, you know. But I want to set us up. It's important to me. So she's going to sell her little house, and I'm going to sell the flat. Hopefully we can buy a reasonable house with extra help from the fund. Chelsea, we thought. God, I'm really happy. I wasn't certain she would say yes. Isn't life marvellous?"

"Yes, isn't it."

"Did you feel like this when you and Mum got engaged?"

"Something like it." I felt ill. I had to change the subject. "What do you think of Sally and Jonathan?"

"They're very serious, that pair. I met someone from the company they work for. Said Sally's done very well. I've always underestimated her, I suppose."

"Brothers often do."

"Yes."

He was drenched in happiness. Sally, Jonathan, his mother, and I were transformed by his joy into far finer figures than we had ever seemed before. "Mum's so good. I know she had more worries than anyone. I thought she'd never unfreeze with Anna. But Mum's wise and kind, and once she saw the inevitability of it all, she became really friendly. Mum's wonderful, don't you think?"

"Indeed I do."

He looked at his watch. "We'd better go back. Dad, thanks for everything. Let's go, the future awaits."

TWENTY-NINE

"Well, she's got him. I knew she would."

"Ingrid! Martyn's the besotted one."

"I know that. I told you that ages ago. But she wanted him too. She wanted him. He suits her."

"So you're happy then."

"Not exactly. But I am bowing to the inevitable." She sighed. "I suppose all mothers feel a bit possessive when their only son decides to marry. Of course, I'm certainly not gaining a daughter. Neither are you."

"What on earth do you mean?"

"Oh, you know . . . lose a son, gain a daughter. Anna has no intention of having a close relationship with me, or you for that matter. Now if Sally's relationship ends where I think it will, Jonathan will be like another son."

"Mm, perhaps."

"Anna's father seemed nice. The mother was a bit cool, I thought. Extraordinary that Martyn hasn't met them. Still, it's all been so quick."

"We've met Wilbur."

"True. The wedding is going to be in June, it's only three months away. Anna's father is coming up to London. He's invited us to lunch next week. I suppose we'll meet the mother just before the wedding. I must say, I'm fascinated to see what they'll turn out to be like. Aren't you?"

"Yes."

Everything is rushing away from me, I thought, as we drove to London. But having bowed my head in resignation and become a victim, I could only watch and suffer, love and wait patiently for my times with Anna. After all, I reflected ruefully, it's more of a life than I ever had before.

THIRTY

Anna's father was the kind of Englishman who impresses all who meet him as a gentleman. The Italians, the French, the Germans, have their aristocrats, but a true English gentleman adheres to a moral code which is subtly practised behind a screen of perfect good manners. Such a man was Charles Anthony Barton. He rose to greet us as we arrived for lunch at Claridge's.

"I'm so sorry my wife is not here to meet you. Our daughter was a little unwell." I remembered the daughter of the second marriage. We apologised for Sally's absence. Her new executive position now demanded executive lunches.

"Do sit down. What would you like to drink, Ingrid? May I call you Ingrid? Champagne perhaps?"

"That would be lovely," said Ingrid.

"Whisky for me, thanks."

Anna and Martyn arrived. She brushed her father's cheek with her lips.

"Father. This is Martyn."

Charles Barton turned to greet my son. His head seemed to jerk as though someone had hit him. In a second he recovered. "It's a great pleasure to meet you, Martyn."

He looked at Anna. "You have kept this young man very secret from us. I'm so pleased for you both."

We sat down slowly.

"Sir. I feel very guilty. I should have driven through the night to beg your permission to marry Anna. But frankly I was concentrating so hard on getting her to say yes, that all else slipped my mind. Please forgive me."

"What a graceful speech! Of course I forgive you. I never expected such a request." He had recovered his poise and he studied Martyn carefully. "Anna, I can see that you are a very lucky girl."

"Now, Father, you should be telling Martyn what a lucky man he is."

"It's obvious Martyn knows that already."

The waiter hovered. We ordered. The pleasantries unique to each such family gathering, and common to all, were exchanged. As the meal wore on I could see that Anna's father, kind though he was, did not really like his daughter very much.

As they kissed goodbye after lunch he tapped her arm for a second, and whispered something to her. I heard her reply:

"I don't agree. It's not that strong . . ." Then she caught me looking at her, and turning to Ingrid she said, "My father thinks Martyn looks rather like my brother, Aston."

"Anna!" Shocked, her father stepped back from her, and bumped into Martyn, who steadied him.

They looked at each other. Martyn spoke. "It must be a terrible shock for you . . . this resemblance . . . if it's there . . ." He paused, distressed.

"You have a kind son." Charles Barton turned to Ingrid. "Forgive the intrusion of sadness into such a happy occasion. It was just a very fleeting resemblance. Anna should not have repeated my comment. I have an appointment I must keep. We will meet again soon. Goodbye, Martyn. I'm pleased, indeed honoured, by the thought of you as my son-in-law. Goodbye, Anna. Be happy, my dear." He shook hands. Frailer and older looking than he seemed only an hour before, he left us.

"Anna, Martyn told me that Aston died when he was very young." Ingrid spoke gently. "If there is a resemblance it must have been an awful shock to your father. Is it a strong resemblance?"

"No, not strong. Perhaps . . . for a second . . . there is a slight resemblance. Martyn has very unusual colouring. So did Aston."

"And so do you," said Ingrid.

"Yes. But it's not so unusual in a woman."

"I dare say it's startling enough, my dear," said Ingrid.

I could see that Ingrid was disconcerted.

Martyn the conciliator stepped in again.

"Mum, we're off to see a house now. All's well. Let's not get this out of perspective. Mum is pale and blonde. Dad is kind of swarthy and dark."

"Thanks."

"I've got Mum's pale skin, and your dark hair. It's not all that uncommon, is it?"

"Of course not. Anna's father was naturally taken aback, that's all."

"Poor Anna. Come along, a-hunting we will go. For a small, sweet house with only happy memories."

Ingrid and I were alone. We ordered another coffee.

"Every time I feel everything will be all right, that girl does something unnerving or strange that makes my

heart go cold. There are people in this world, innocent
in their own way, who cause damage. Anna is one. She
is going to harm Martyn, I'm certain. My first reactions
were right. They always are. Oh, why didn't I intervene
earlier?"

"Really, Ingrid, what are you so upset about? Her father noticed a resemblance to Anna's brother—that's not
so terrible, is it?"

The calming and soothing of others is always the best
antidote to one's own panic and dismay.

"What happened to that boy? I'm certain you know
the full story. Martyn told you. Didn't he?"

"No."

"There was a tragedy. She's linked to it in some way."

"Ingrid, our son is marrying a beautiful, intelligent
woman. Her father is clearly a very nice man. Her stepfather is charming. We haven't met her mother yet, but
I'm sure we'll like her too. Her brother died when
young. Anna is more complex and perhaps less easy as a
daughter-in-law than you would have liked. But that's
all. Now stop. You're worrying unnecessarily."

"Maybe you're right. This has just confirmed all my
prejudices against her."

"Exactly! If you'd been relaxed about her from the
beginning, this incident would have meant nothing."

"Mm."

But behind my words lay my own stalking fear. What
dangerous pattern is being reworked here? Sudden fear
for my family engulfed me. Liar! cried the policeman in
my heart. Liar! The only fear that grips and eats your
belly is the fear of losing her. You cannot win her out-
right, each day that passes teaches you that more clearly.

But you hold on. Because you know there is no life for you without her.

I smiled at Ingrid, and with many reassurances, I helped her on her way to Hell.

I caught sight of us as we passed through the lobby, an elegant blonde woman of a certain age, and her companion, vaguely familiar perhaps, well dressed, strong good face. Of the evil in my soul there was not a trace.

THIRTY-ONE

"Evidently yesterday was a good day for the lovers. The house was exactly what they wanted."

"Good."

Each day now revealed to me my treachery and its desperate ways with ferocious clarity.

That evening, dinner with Ingrid had a brooding quietness which I knew concealed her anger.

"I rang Martyn today. He didn't like my enquiries. But for once I was a pushy Mum. I'm not normally, am I?"

"No. You're normally very discreet."

"He's renting his flat to someone at work, he says the rental will be handy for living expenses. Anna's mews house goes on the market immediately. Martyn thinks it will sell easily. He intends using part of the trust fund to cover the cost of the new house. It's been empty for a couple of months—needs some work, evidently. They can move in after completion. They want a quiet, family wedding at the end of next month. All very neat, very fast, quite clinical almost. So no Hartley wedding. A Registry Office affair and then a family lunch. They're adamant. Evidently Anna's mother is coming over a week before the wedding. At least we'll meet her before the actual ceremony. We'll have to invite her to lunch or dinner or something. Let's hope Sally gives us a more traditional wedding. Apart from all my worries, I feel quite cheated."

"Sally will do everything the way you hope. She's a treasure really, a wise, pretty, conventional middle-class girl."

"Thank God for Sally! Martyn's changed so much, don't you think? He's very different. Oh, for that endless stream of lovely blondes. The Sunday lunch brigade."

"I think they're gone for good."

"Yes, Anna's the kiss of death to all that."

The phrase hung in the air for a second too long.

"I asked Martyn about Aston."

"Yes? What did he say?"

"Says it was all very sad, that Anna had told him ages ago that Aston had committed suicide. He was terribly young, I gather. I read an article the other day, it's not all that uncommon. Oh dear, I don't mean it to sound like that but . . ."

"I know what you mean. It's not unheard of. Puberty, dawning adolescence—it's very hard for some boys."

"Martyn was quite angry with me by the end of the conversation. It was very much 'This is my life, I know what I'm doing.' I've been replaced by Anna . . . she is his priority now . . . just as it should be." She looked at me quizzically. "Our own times are a bit fraught at the moment, don't you think? You and me."

"A little. It will pass."

"If I didn't know you so well, I could now be persuaded you were having an affair."

"Could you? I'm almost flattered."

"Well, don't be. I couldn't bear it. Frankly, I wouldn't bear it." She challenged me with her eyes.

"I'm duly warned," I said. The voice inside said, I'm not having an affair—not an affair. I'm consumed body and soul and mind. My whole existence is geared to only one thing, my time with Anna. My life before her was an efficient lie, in which you, Ingrid, played your part. There will be no life after Anna. There will be no life after her.

With a weary smile of self-pity, I went to my study to work for an hour. I wanted to give Ingrid time to slip into bed and sleep, without further conversation. A new ritual was being established. In its early days it required total discipline.

I rang the next day. "Anna, I've got to see you."

"I know. I was going to ring you."

"Your place at three thirty?"

"Yes."

She opened the door, and I walked after her to the bedroom. From a bedside table drawer she took a framed photograph of a young boy. A long, angular, almost sullen face glared back at me. There was a resemblance to Martyn, undoubtedly. But as Anna had said, it was fleeting.

"You see. It's nothing, it's nothing."

"Then why did you announce to all and sundry the remark your father made?"

She put the photograph back in the drawer, which she closed carefully. "I was angry with him. Very angry. He should have said nothing."

"Did you notice the resemblance when you first saw Martyn?"

"Of course. For a second . . . of course."

"Is that part of it? Part of your attraction to Martyn?"

"No. No. I want to live a normal married life with him."

"What a strange way of putting it."

She smiled. "You pry. But not as much as you used to. You're changing."

"I'm carrying my burden. I too have chosen my life, and the way I want to live it."

She brought her face close to mine and whispered, "Everything. Always."

All her features, enlarged from this perspective, and almost ugly, devoured me. We fell around the room, against or below wood and glass and velvet. I became obsessed that day, that in the curve of her spine I would find bones that would unlock a secret way to her. Finally, we became still, her face crushed against the pattern on the silken wall, and my stomach pressed hard to the small of her back. After the moment of ecstasy, her face fell back into its old perspectives. And all I was, or ever would be, had been revealed to me again.

As I left, she said:

"I have a gift for you." She handed me a small box. "I keep my promises. Remember that. Forget the rest." She closed my hand around it. "I planned this, a little time ago." She opened the door, and I slipped out.

I walked to a small café. I needed to sit somewhere quietly, while I opened the box. Inside there were two keys. Flat C.15. Welbeck Way, W1. I hailed a taxi, and arrived in minutes.

Behind the imposing facade of a period building lay a dark green marble hall, from which ascended galleried landings with carved balustrades. A small stained-glass dome shed an eerie light on marble, wood, and pale grey walls. On each floor two flats faced each other from opposite sides of the well.

The flat itself was really only a large room, with a bathroom and kitchen. The room was barely furnished, a large table, some chairs, and in a corner a small double bed. Under empty bookcases was a low glass table. On the table was a note. 'This room will contain nothing but us. A world within a world. I shall visit it to know your wishes. For in this world I have created, you rule and I am your slave. I will wait at the times you designate. Being obedient, I will always be there.'

Beside the letter was an antique leather-bound diary, and a quill and an antique ink stand. The diary fell open at the day's date. Folded on the page was a long green silk ribbon, and underneath was written, 'And he came into his kingdom.' I flicked the empty pages forward and found an entry ten days ahead which said 'Anna waits, twelve till two.'

I walked into the bathroom. It was stacked with soap, toothbrushes, toothpaste, tissues, towels. The kitchen had two cups and saucers, two glasses, tea, coffee, and whisky. The fridge contained only bottled water. I looked for colour. The carpet in the lounge was the colour of dark wine. There were no curtains, only a dark blind on the single large window that looked down onto a square of green. I pulled the blind and a half darkness fell upon me. I treasured my kingdom. And I was pleased.

I bound up the diary with the green ribbon and placed a note under the ribbon which read, 'Open on the twentieth, between twelve and two.'

I left.

Later that night Ingrid and I parted after a dinner dominated by talk of the wedding, to our ritual safe places—the study for me, the bedroom for her. I felt the keys in my pocket as I sat down to work, as a poor man might feel a gem he had just stolen. A gem which would transform his life.

My days were filled with my Committee meetings and my nights with snippets from Ingrid concerning the wedding, the reception, the honeymoon. Oh, the attractive, winning, and futile ways in which we bind woman and man. In order to tame the only bond that matters.

And between twelve and two on the day appointed I slipped the key in the door to my kingdom. Anna, real and magnificent, lay on the floor; the diary was on her stomach. She smiled as I undid the ribbon.

When it was time to go she wrote in the diary. I saw the time—four to six—and that the date was the day before her wedding. She took a new ribbon—blue—and wound it round and round the diary. Stroking my face she said, "Everything. Always. Remember."

THIRTY-TWO

Anna and her mother, Elizabeth, sat side by side on the sofa in our sitting room. Anna as always was quiet, controlled. Her mother was petite, almost birdlike. The dark eyes and hair she'd passed on to Anna were a disconcerting counterpoint to all that was different about them.

A tired air of practised vivacity hung about her. I guessed that it was habit that produced the falsely bright smile, the too-quickly friendly response.

Yes, her journey had been exhausting. But she had something wonderful to look forward to. She answered my queries concerning her flight. Then she turned to Ingrid.

"Do you like travelling, Ingrid?"

"No, not a lot."

"Wilbur is flying in on Thursday." He'd told her all about Martyn and his marvellous family. Patting Anna's hand, she said, "Anna doesn't write often enough—do you, Anna?"

"No."

"Phone calls are less personal, contrary to what people think. I always reveal myself more in letters. But Anna never reveals herself much anyway. She was always very secretive, weren't you, dear?" She patted Anna's hand again. "Do you know, when you and Aston" (she pronounced the name as though she were in some way unfamiliar with it) "were small, you were always secretive." Turning to Martyn. "You know about Aston, I'm sure, Martyn. You look a little bit like him. Did Anna tell you that?" It now seemed an innocent remark. Elizabeth gave Martyn a quick nervous smile.

"Yes, indeed. Anna did mention it." Martyn's voice was full of kindness.

"When they were small I felt sure that Aston and Anna had formed a little secret society. They had code words, strange signals—all designed to make it very difficult for parents." She beamed at Anna. "You were very naughty really, weren't you?"

"Naughty!" Martyn laughed. "I can't imagine it."

"Oh yes. Very, very naughty. I like to think of those times. Though they lead me to much sadder thoughts."

I could see there was a vulnerability about her, a sweetness which was still attractive. Two very clever men had married her. Her vivacity, her prettiness, the chic little body must have had the power to dazzle in years gone by. I guessed her face had gone from the prettiness of youth to a faded version of itself years later, without the self-knowledge or wisdom which might have made her beautiful in her maturity. She was, I thought, a not very intelligent woman, who had been wholly out of her depth with her children. I conceived a sudden dislike of Aston, and I did not warm to Elizabeth's picture of Anna as a child. Perhaps that is her mother's great strength, I thought—she elicits pity. As she chatted on, happily undermining her daughter, it was Anna sitting quietly beside her who seemed the malevolent one.

"But this is a marvellous time," she continued. "I'm so happy for Anna. Now tell me, have you decided on a honeymoon?"

"We're going to Paris for a week."

Her mother looked concerned.

"Yes. Well, Paris has always been your favourite city. You like it too, Martyn?"

"Very much. It's Anna's idea. I must say, I'm looking forward to it. We went there some time ago. It was all rather unfortunate because Anna wasn't too well. We had to come back early."

"Oh dear, oh dear. And Paris holds such happy memories for you, Anna, doesn't it?" She looked at Anna, who now betrayed a sullen anger.

"Mm."

"Why?" asked Ingrid.

"Anna's first romance" (she seemed to select the word carefully) "was in Paris. We left Rome after . . . the tragedy, and spent some time in Paris. Peter had just started his studies, indeed he still lives there. He's married now . . . poor boy, it was a hopeless failure. His mother tells me he used often to come to London. He recently sold the little flat he kept here. Have you seen him at all? I think it's so nice when a friendship remains after the romance is over. Don't you agree?" She turned to Ingrid.

"Mother . . . please," Anna interjected.

"Oh dear! Am I being indiscreet again? Anna, you look rather angry with me."

"No, Mother, not angry."

"Martyn, I'm sure you had romances before Anna."

"One or two."

"All blondes," said Sally, who had just arrived. "Hundreds of blondes paraded through this very room. My darling brother was a real Don Juan."

"But those days are over, I assure you." Martyn smiled at Elizabeth. "We are very happy."

"I can see that! Anna, you're a very lucky girl. Oh, Anna, now stop being cross with me. Peter's mother and I keep in touch. It was a perfectly innocent remark."

"What does Peter do?" I asked.

"After three generations of civil servants, he surprised everyone and became a psychiatrist. He has a very successful practice in Paris. French is his second language, and he says sometimes the discipline of another language reveals the truth more clearly." She laughed, then she said, "I sound like Wilbur."

"Why did he come to London so much?"

"Work, I suppose. I don't really know. It's on my mind because of my last letter from his mother. She mentioned he'd sold his little flat quite suddenly and . . ."

Anna stood up. With a quiet "Excuse me" she left the room. There was an embarrassed silence.

"Oh dear! I wish I'd never started this conversation. It's of no importance whatsoever. Anna's secrecy never ceases to amaze me."

"Maybe it's a defence," said Martyn.

"A defence against what?"

"I can't imagine," replied Martyn.

Clever Martyn. Now you see through her too—this lethal mother slowly revealing herself. No wonder Aston and Anna had closed themselves up against her in their own secret world. And after Aston's death no wonder they all separated—unable to avoid the bloodletting or to cleanse the guilt, to face up to their individual culpability.

So silence, separation, and sadness had become a way of life. There were new marriages, new lives, new loves, to take them away, away from everything that went before. Yet they were still trapped—each of them—in the unresolved agonies of long ago.

The evening came to an end, with everyone less happy than when it had begun. As Martyn started the engine, and Anna held the door open for Elizabeth, I walked Anna's mother down the short path to the iron gate and to the car. "What's Peter's second name?" I asked quietly, carefully judging the distance to Martyn and Anna. "I have a friend in Paris who has a serious problem."

"Calderon. Dr. Peter Calderon. He's in the book. Don't let Anna know I've told you. She'd be incensed. Wilbur sent a writer friend of his to Peter once. He was very helpful." We were at the car. We said our goodbyes. "Until next Saturday."

They sped away.

"Strange woman. She's a complete contrast to Anna. Isn't she?" asked Ingrid.

"I rather liked her," said Sally. "She's more open and chatty than Anna."

"Well, that's putting it mildly," said Ingrid. "So now we've met them all. Mother, father, stepfather—not the stepmother yet. I suppose I've got a bigger family now. It certainly doesn't feel like it. Probably never will. Not with this family anyway." She sighed. "It will be different with Jonathan. We already know the Robinsons. Do we see another wedding looming on the horizon?" Ingrid teased Sally.

"Well, I certainly haven't been asked yet."

"You will be, you will be. And let me tell you now, I

want a large white wedding followed by a conventional reception at Hartley. Promise me." Ingrid hugged the blushing Sally.

"I promise, Mum, I promise."

With thoughts about weddings and children, mothers and fathers, we put the day down. We went our separate ways to our rooms, and to sleep.

THIRTY-THREE

"Dr. Peter Calderon?"

"Oui."

"I'm a friend of Anna Barton's. I'd like to come and see you."

"Why?"

"I think it would be helpful."

"To whom?"

"To me."

"Did Anna tell you to ring me?"

"No."

"What kind of friend are you?"

"I'm Martyn's father."

There was a short silence.

"Ah yes, Martyn. Anna has told me of her decision to marry."

The words "decision to marry" seemed awkward and strangely formal.

"This is clearly not a professional call. I would simply like to say that I wish Anna and Martyn a most happy marriage. I feel we should draw this conversation to an end." He paused. "I do not go to London anymore. Anna rarely visits Paris."

"Is Anna a patient of yours?"

"I don't have to answer that, but I will. No."

"But you understand her in a different way from most people—because of your training."

"Not quite. I would say the person who best understands Anna is the man she is going to marry. Your son. I gather he allows her mysteries, her secrets, and perhaps her other loves."

"Other loves?"

"Yes, always."

There was a silence.

"Anna has never spoken of you to me."

"Why should she? I'm just Martyn's father."

"Clearly, you are a most unusual father. But then you also have a most unusual son. And this is a very strange conversation." He sighed. "Anna provokes strange conversations."

"Why didn't you marry Anna?"

"Oh, God. Shall I answer that? I could not give her what she needed."

"Which is what?"

"Freedom. Freedom to be bound always to those she loves, to all of those whom she loves. It requires great reserves of character and intelligence, and of course great love, to be able to give her that."

"Or perhaps just a refusal to face the truth about her."

"Oh, I feel your son has quietly faced many truths about Anna. In fact I'm certain of it."

"Why?"

"Because Martyn and I have met."

"When?"

"I will not say more."

"Why didn't you tell me in the beginning?"

"Who knows where a conversation may end? As ours is doing now, with another mystery, which will, on investigation, reveal yet another concealed truth. No wonder I am fulfilled in my profession. Now goodbye. Good luck to you and to your son. Please do not ring me again."

Martyn, my brilliant boy, so you got to Peter Calderon before me. And what has all your cleverness, and all your love brought you? Not all of Anna. I have all of Anna when she comes to me. Perhaps in truth I do not want the rest of her life and time. Why ask for more? Peter asked for more and lost everything. The flat in Welbeck Way had been his, of course. I understood that now.

It should have mattered. It didn't matter.

THIRTY-FOUR

I do not have an elegant body. I am too powerfully built for grace. I dress with care. I present myself to the world in my dark grey flannel suits, white shirt, and wine tie (I order in bulk) in the guise of an elegant man. I have always dressed in this way. My leisurewear also tends to a tasteful correctness that has been helpful in formalising the distance I like to keep from others. I am not casual, easy, or particularly approachable.

On the day before the wedding, as I too walked towards my new life with Anna (for that was how I saw it), I knew the burden which had weighed so heavily on my heart had now become bearable. I had accepted that my life would continue on a dangerous edge.

At the flat, Anna was waiting for me. A suitcase sat like an ornament on the glass table.

"I told Martyn I wanted this afternoon and night to myself. I will arrive at the Registry Office from my secret place. After you leave—I hope you can stay longer than we planned—I shall lie here in this room and dream of all my lives. I am happy. I simply cannot believe it. I am happy. I have never been happy, not since childhood. Now I am. It's an extraordinary feeling. Have you been happy?"

"I just don't know. Perhaps I was. It's sad, but I really can't remember." I sighed. "It seems so unimportant."

She opened the small suitcase. Carefully she took out a cream dress and a tiny hat. She put them into an empty cupboard.

"That is for tomorrow," she smiled. "This afternoon, and this evening is for you."

As her dress fell from her, I knew her tribute in the way the dark silken cord passed between her legs, and the way in which its undulating colour wove itself around her breasts. She pointed to a dark bruise and whispered, " 'Giving herself a voluntary wound, here in the thigh.' You see, I too can prove my strength and my fidelity."

I eased her gently to the floor. Leaving my elegant disguise on the sofa I became myself.

I told her dreams in language she alone could understand. A powerful goddess, she whispered yes, yes, through the hours of her imprisonment. In her omnipotence she ruled her enslaved master. I found in her suitcase hand-embroidered ribbon and wound it round and round until she could not see. Then I wanted silence. I found soft cotton nuggets of withdrawal, and once they were in place we moved in a world of absolute silence.

A pulse in her stomach seemed to beat a soundless rhythm on her skin as she lay on the floor. My mouth, in predatory pursuit, pressed down, and with my tongue I tried to catch its butterfly movements. In vain.

My fist kneaded the self-inflicted dark blue bruise on her thigh. Powerless to erase it, I forced its darkness to spread like a stain towards the clotted hair parted by the silken cord between her legs.

As the door gave way to him, for a second I was the only one who saw Martyn. With frantic fingers, I tore the silence from our ears. Anna cried, "What is it? What is it?" I pulled the ribbon from her eyes, and in a second we both could hear him whisper: "Impossible. Impossible. Possible."

Framed in the doorway he seemed to rock forwards and backwards on the narrow landing.

I rose to help him. He raised his arms above his head as if to ward off a terrible blow. Then, like a child moving backwards, robotically, step by step from undreamed-of evil, and gazing at the face that had destroyed him, he fell silently over the banisters to his death on the marble floor below.

The power of my body as I held him in my arms, his neck as awkward as a broken stem, was useless in its strength. Where, where is the softness that could have cradled him? Breasts are needed, and roundness and softness, for the dead bodies of our children, as we hold them to us in the wild truthfulness of our grief. The hardness of my chest gave his face no place to hide. My muscled arms felt obscene and threatening, as they tried to gather and shape the brokenness of his body to me.

The empty lobby became a marble pit, into which people threw questions of hope in shocked voices.

"Shall I call a doctor?"

"Can I help?"

"I've called the police."

"Shall I bring a blanket? For you? For the body?" I realised I was naked.

"Is he dead? Oh, is he dead?"

And then Anna slowly walked towards us. Dressed and combed and hideously calm, she said, "It's over. It's all over." Touching me lightly on the shoulder and looking at Martyn without pity, she almost glided towards the door, and disappeared into the night.

Others now were in the pit. They formed a silent circle round us, the naked man and his jeaned and sweatered beautiful dead son. A woman threw a red stole over me. It fell on my body, to the sound of the door slamming behind Anna. More noise, and then a policeman parted the group without having to say a word. Kneeling quietly beside me he said:

"He's dead, I'm afraid."

"Yes—he died instantly."

We looked at each other.

"It's . . . it's . . . ?"

"Yes."

"And who is the young man?"

"He is my son, Martyn."

The doctor and ambulance men knelt down beside me. Another policeman quietly asked the small group to move with him to the back of the lobby. I heard their whispers like a soft, sad song in the background. It was hard to let Martyn's body go from my arms. But the doctor was gentle and the ambulance men were discreet and efficient. Then it was only me, and the policeman, and we were mounting the stairs towards the flat. The door was open. Apart from my now neatly folded clothes, there was no sign of how the time had been before the crashing of the door.

"May I dress?"

The policeman looked at my naked body clutching the red stole and he nodded. "We will need to take a statement . . . later, sir. We'd like to take it at the Police Station."

"Yes, of course. I must talk to my wife. It's vital I talk to her."

"I understand that, sir." He looked around. "There seems to be no phone."

"No."

"Who owns this flat, sir?"

"My son's fiancée."

"And what is her name?"

"Anna Barton."

"Was she the young lady who left as we arrived?"

The policeman who had been talking to the group downstairs had joined us.

"Yes."

"She can't have lived here long. There's nothing here."

"She doesn't live here."

They waited. I had finished dressing.

"We know it was an accident, sir. Two witnesses saw your son fall backwards over the banisters. They confirm you didn't touch him."

"No."

"What were you doing, sir?"

"I was with Miss Barton."

"Your son's fiancée?"

"Yes."

"Sir. I must ask this question. You were naked . . ."

"Miss Barton and I were making . . ." I stopped.

It was not a word I had used before.

"We understand, sir."

"Your son was unaware of this until tonight?"

"Of course."

"How did he know you were here?"

"I don't know. I simply don't know."

"And where is Miss Barton now?"

"I don't know. She just walked out. Just walked past us."

"She will be in a state of shock. We had better try to trace her."

"I don't know where she'd go. Maybe back to their house."

"Whose house, sir?"

"Anna's and Martyn's. They had just bought a house. They were engaged."

"And when did they plan to marry, sir?"

"Tomorrow."

There was a long silence. "Let's go to the station now, sir."

I rang Ingrid from the station. Sally answered.

"You don't have to say anything. Anna's been here."

"Oh, God! Where is she now?"

"At the Wellington with Wilbur."

"Wilbur?"

"Yes. He had a heart attack this afternoon. Martyn rang earlier, he was trying to find Anna." She paused. "I told Anna about Wilbur and she left immediately."

"Is your mother there?"

"Yes. Don't ask to talk to her. Not yet."

"Sally. Oh, Sally."

"Mother and I are going to see Martyn's body. She wants to desperately."

I turned to the policeman. "To which hospital did they take my son's body?"

"The Middlesex."

I told Sally. "Now listen, please, please don't go. I will make a formal identification tonight. I swear I will take you tomorrow. Persuade your mother to wait. It's most important. Please do this, Sally."

"I'll try, I'll try. Anna's mad—you know that, don't you?"

"No. No, Sally, she's not mad."

"She had her suitcase with her. She said she would see Wilbur and then she would go to Paris. 'I was all ready for the flight anyway,' she said, 'for my honeymoon.' She smiled at me. Can you believe that? She smiled at me. If she's not mad, she's evil."

"Oh, Sally, Sally, she's neither of those things."

"What is she then? She has led both you and Martyn to destruction."

"She told your mother everything?"

"I don't know. There are some things Mother won't say. I can't ask really. But I can guess."

"I don't think you can, Sally. I will come home later."

"Don't. Please."

"I will, Sally. I must. Later." I put the phone down.

"My wife knows."

"Yes sir. I could tell."

I sat in a small office with a tall grey-haired man, Inspector Doonan. He had a weary kindness about him. Kindness was perhaps his last resort when confronted by the endlessly repeating pattern of human folly. How lucky I was to be with Inspector Doonan.

I made my statement. He had some questions.

"How long has your relationship with . . . ?"

"Anna. Four months."

"How long have you known her?"

"It started immediately. Within days of our meeting."

"Your son had no idea?"

"No one had."

"No one?"

"Well one person. Anna's stepfather, Wilbur. Oh God, he's had a heart attack. He's in the Wellington. That's why Martyn was searching for Anna. May I phone?"

"Yes sir, of course." He went to the door and someone got the Wellington on the phone. I established which suite Wilbur was in, and spoke to the Senior Sister. It was a brief and reassuring conversation. Wilbur was out of intensive care—three days in hospital and then he must take a long rest. It had been a very mild attack.

"How did your son know you were both at this address?"

"He didn't. I just don't understand it. He didn't know about this flat."

"He didn't have a key. He forced the lock," said Inspector Doonan.

"That's what brought the Thompsons to the landing upstairs." The young policeman spoke.

"The Thompsons?"

"The witnesses who saw Martyn fall."

"Ah."

"Do you think Miss Barton was careless? Maybe she left the address in a book?"

"No. She was not a careless person."

"Where is she now? We will have to talk to her."

"Paris. She's on her way to Paris, to Peter. Peter! This was his flat originally. Martyn may have called him when he couldn't think where Anna would go. Peter! He must have talked to Peter in Paris."

"Who's Peter?"

"She said she wanted to be alone before the wedding. Just turn up from a secret address."

"Slow down, sir. It's confusing."

"Can I ring him?"

"Who? Peter?"

"Yes."

"In Paris?"

"I'll pay."

"It's not that, sir." He sighed. "Do you know the number?"

"Yes." Inspector Doonan handed me the phone.

"Peter?"

"Oui."

"It's Martyn's father."

"I know. Anna rang. She's on her way here. There's nothing to say. I'm desperately sorry."

"Did you give him the address?"

"Yes."

"I thought so."

"I didn't know you were there. I thought it was where Anna would go to think. To be quiet before tomorrow. When Martyn rang . . . desperate . . . because of Wilbur, I told him. We were friends, in a way, Martyn and I."

"In a way we are friends."

"In a way."

"Anna may have to come back."

"I will explain to her."

"The police know it was an accident, but she will have to make a statement."

"Sure, I understand."

"I must go now."

"Goodbye."

"Goodbye."

I made my statement.

"We'll drive you home, sir. But first we need a formal identification."

We went to the hospital. I made the identification. There is nothing to say. I will not speak of this.

It was after one o'clock when I let myself into the house. The door of Sally's old bedroom opened. Her groggy face appeared. I motioned her back and whispered: "Your mother." Sally closed the door.

I walked towards a light. Ingrid was waiting for me in the kitchen. It was not a kitchen designed for this kind of pain. Its shiny surfaces and high whiteness were more likely to intensify agony than to abate it. There were no dark corners and no soft wood to absorb the screams—whether silent or not. Black-suited, with her back to me, she bore for a second a most terrible resemblance to Anna. She swung round to me. The shock of her face brought vomit to my mouth. I grabbed a towel; the sick was an old familiar odour to me. She handed me a glass of water.

Touching her face she said, "I did it to stop the pain, with this." She held up a small blood-spattered white towel with a knot in it. Her face was streaked with blood. The swelling of her cheeks made her face look as though all its outlines had been raised, while her eyes seemed to have been forced back into tiny pools of black in some lumpen moonscape.

"The pain was devouring me. This helped."

She picked up the towel again and lashed herself. A spurt of blood dropped into the glass on the table. Some image of Anna came obscenely to me. Her face, I thought, had always had something swollen—indelicate—about it. Perhaps that was the key? Anna had no delicate features that could be harmed by the brutality of kisses that must save a life.

Ingrid's face, previously so delicately shaped, so fine of cheekbone, so small, so pale of eye, had always seemed to say: 'Be careful. I can be broken.' Her body too, so long and so thin with subtle curves of breast and hip, had spelled taboo to anything other than most gentle love. I had searched for pleasure as carefully as one would examine a rare piece of porcelain from some distant land.

Ingrid sat down opposite me.

"You are not an evil man," she said. "And I am not a foolish woman."

We looked at each other, a man and a woman, total strangers. Tomorrow or the next day we would bury our son.

"It is clear to me, you and . . . Anna"—she sighed rather than spoke her name—"you could do nothing. You are not an evil man." Her swollen lips and the tears in her throat gave a thickness to her voice. The words 'evil man' had a heavy falling rhythm, as though a drum were beating a single word: 'Evilman, Evilman, Evilman.'

"When you knew . . ." she said, "when you knew you were lost . . ." She paused, and seemed to sway, so that the strange new shape and violent colour of her face became like some hideous mobile. ". . . you should have killed yourself. You should have killed yourself. You know how. It would have been easy for you. You know how."

"Yes. I suppose I do."

"Not now," she said, "not now. No, you coward, not now. Stay. Stay on this world. Stay on and give me a little joy. Why, oh why, didn't you kill yourself? You knew how to do it."

"I honestly never thought of it. I never even thought of it." I felt like some child who could so easily have saved himself from a severe beating. But who had simply never thought of the obvious solution.

"Aston did that," I whispered.

"Aston?"

"Her brother."

"I had forgotten about him. Aston . . . and now Martyn. Oh God, that evil girl." She screamed at me. "I could have buried you and lived. Do you understand? I could have buried you, and lived. Even knowing what you had done, I could have buried you. And lived. And loved. The pain would have been bearable. This pain is unbearable. It is unbearable." She started to whip her face again. I ran behind her and grabbed her. It was an uneven struggle, and was quickly over.

I placed her in a chair. "Don't move," I whispered. I went to my cabinet, and came back with some tranquillisers.

"No," she said flatly. "And no and no and no."

"It is essential," I said.

"Essential for whom?" She rasped. "For you. Because for once you don't know what to do . . . do you, doctor? I only want what I can never have. I want my son back. Give me my son back. Give him back to me. Now. Give him back to me now."

"Ingrid, listen to me. Martyn is dead. He is gone for ever. For ever. His life is over. Listen to me, Ingrid. Listen to me. I brought this death into being. Let me carry it. I will never release myself from his death, or fly away from it. Let it slip towards me, Ingrid. Push it towards me, push his death towards me. Breathe deeply, Ingrid, breathe deeply. You will live after this. Push Martyn's death towards me. You will live. Give him to me now. Give me his death."

I took her to the table, and laid her on it. She drew her legs towards her chest as though to give birth. Tears ran stinging down her cheeks. The buttons of her jacket burst under her convulsions, and her sobbing, and the writhing of her body. "Give his death to me now, Ingrid."

"Oh Martyn, Martyn, Martyn," she cried. Then a terrible silent scream was followed by a sigh so deep that I knew it was over. Something flew towards me and seemed to invade me.

She lay on the table quietly weeping. The tears flowed, softly bathing her bruises, gathering the blood from her face. Tears and blood almost formed a garland around her neck, that broke into rivulets of pale rose and flowed towards her breasts.

"I am going to wash," she said.

I led her to the bathroom. We moved slowly, my friend and I. Perhaps I had some skills that might yet send her peacefully into the rest of her life.

I ran the bath, and added one of her oils. She loosened her hair, which had incongruously remained throughout in an elegant chignon. Her hair clips, and her years of expertise, allowed it to survive such chaos, like some small token of normality.

I helped her undress as one would a child. She slid into the water and under. The oil on her body and hair was like a magician's unguent remedy. Endlessly she lay there, or she slid under the water, repeating as though to some unheard rhythm a ritual acrobatic of survival.

I sat on the floor concentrating all my energies towards her. With a power I did not know I possessed, I eliminated every other thought from my mind. Sometimes I let more hot water flow into the bath. Sometimes I let some water flow away. She did not seem to notice me as she surfaced, and slipped under again. Finally she said, "I'd like to sleep."

I wrapped her in a towel and patted her dry. Then, I tried to slip a nightgown over her. She shook her head, and slid between the sheets. She was asleep in seconds. I sat by the window, and looked into the night. There was a full moon in the starless sky. I thought how rarely I had noticed such things. Some deep failure of the soul perhaps. An inherited emptiness. A nothingness passed from generation to generation. A flaw in the psyche, discovered only by those who suffer by it.

Images of Martyn as a child consumed me—one particularly, a running turn of the head as I called to him; the glory of his laughter framed by a golden summer day. I shut my eyes slowly to draw a curtain over it. I had a funeral to prepare for. I must now make arrangements for a funeral.

I found some writing paper and started my list. Obituary notices, *The Times, Telegraph*. I feared that other announcements—less gentle—would be made by messengers of death, into the unheeding morning lives of people I would never know.

There would be innuendo in the sleazier papers and perhaps a simple statement of the tragedy in the others. For myself I did not care. To preserve the dignity of

Martyn's life seemed suddenly vital to me. Could I do anything? Agitation, terrible agitation, made me jerk my shoulders and my head in short mechanical movements. God! I can't go into a state of shock. I must hold on. I slipped from the room. I swallowed some Diazepam and went back to my list—authorities, coffin, church service, flowers, music.

Ingrid stirred. I glanced at my watch. Hours had passed. How could that be possible? The moon was gone. Dawn, it was almost today. Today was here. So now Martyn had died yesterday. Martyn died this day last week, last month, last year. It is ten years ago today since Martyn died. It is twenty years ago. When would I cease to mark it? When, oh when, would I die?

Ingrid moaned. Today, and its pain, was implacably eating its way into her sleep. I watched the movements of her body change from anger to defeat. Finally she sank back in an agony of submission. Her eyes, suddenly awake, knew in a second: 'It's true, isn't it.' I helped her from her bed. We did not speak.

Slowly and silently she walked towards the bathroom and carefully shut the door. I turned to the window and watched the day approach and lengthen. Cars and people and sounds filled some strange area of consciousness. The milk van rounding the corner seemed like a space vehicle, proceeding historically across a newly discovered planet.

I knew some split had occurred. A ravine had opened. I knew that for me the real world must stay in a new and vivid focus. The separate automatic part of my existence was the one in which I would have to function. In the next few days I must inhabit this part of me totally. The other area must lie dormant, to be lived in later, possibly for ever.

Fear gripped me. Start now, start now, in this dimension. Stare at cars. Hear sounds. Focus on the milk van. Look! It has jerked suddenly to a stop outside.

Ingrid came from the bathroom. Transformed. Her chignon was again shaped to its pleated beauty. Her face from which the swelling had subsided through the night had the masklike immobility of a perfect discreet maquillage. She walked into the room, cloaked in the artificial perfection with which already beautiful women arm themselves against the world. She was also naked.

The intimacy of marriage had never dulled the sharpness of that image. She stood in front of me and said, "What a pity that we ever met."

"What of Sally? There is still Sally."

"Yes. Yes. Sally. But you know, Martyn was the one for me. There is always just one person really. Anna, I suppose, for you?"

I sighed.

"How lucky for you, she's not dead. Is she? Anna is . . . Anna . . . to use the vernacular . . . is a survivor, is she not? Were you ever in love with me?"

"Yes. It seemed so right," I said.

"And this." She motioned towards her body. "And this?"

"You are extraordinarily beautiful."

"I know that. My God! Do you think I don't know that?" She turned towards the full-length mirror. "I have," she said, "a beautiful face, look at it. Look at my body. My breasts are small but still lovely. My waist and hips are slender." She drew a line with her hands down towards her genitals. "And what about this? This part of me at the top of my elegant, elegant legs. Tell me about all this beauty? Not enough, was it? Not enough! Its failure has cost me Martyn."

She turned to me. Now, reflected in the full-length mirror, were the slender lines of her back and the incongruous, frightening perfection of her chignon. "You should have died," she said quietly. "You should have died. My God, you never really seemed alive anyway."

"You are absolutely right on both counts. I should have died. But I didn't think of it. I never was really alive to anything until Anna."

"Perhaps after all you are an evil man. Well, you've worked your horror in my life. For a second, just a second you understand, I thought of making love to you."

I looked startled. She laughed. A short, bitter, brittle laugh. "Looking at you I can see how totally irrelevant I have become. I will take considerable strength from that." She opened a drawer and slipped into her underwear. Then she put on a black dress of such stark simplicity that she seemed an icon of useless beauty, form without power.

I heard Edward arrive. Ingrid ran down to him. Edward held his daughter tight to him. The devastation in his face was terrible. "Oh, my Ingrid," he whispered, "my dearest, darling, darling Ingrid, my poor child."

"Oh, Daddy."

I stood paralysed for a second. It was not Ingrid who called to Edward, but Sally to me.

Standing at the door of the room she whispered, "Oh, Daddy."

I moved towards her. But suddenly she said, "No! No," and turned and went down the stairs, as though just to look at me had hurt her.

I followed slowly.

"Sally, you were wonderful last night." Edward spoke. "It must have been very hard for you. Sally told me, you know." Edward nodded towards me. "Very hard on the girl . . . very hard."

"Sally's very brave. Good morning, sir." Jonathan was in the hall. "I'm desperately sorry." His voice trailed off.

"Can we talk . . . privately?" We went into the study. "I'm going to take charge of ringing the Registry Office and the hotel," he said. "Everyone, except Anna's parents. Lucky it was just family . . . Oh God, that sounds awful . . . you know what I mean."

"I'll ring Anna's mother. Wilbur has just had a mild heart attack. It is vital he is handled properly. Her father is at the Savoy, I believe. I'll ring him too."

"Sir, I'll work from Sally's room, if that's all right."

I nodded. The request was a courtesy, all the more appreciated.

"You love Sally?"

"Very much."

"I'm very glad. I'd like to say, I'm glad it's you."

"Thank you, sir."

I rang Anna's mother.

"I was about to ring you," she said. "There was nothing I could say or do last night. I've waited since dawn to ring you."

"You know?"

"Oh yes."

"Anna?"

"Yes. She came to see Wilbur. Once outside in the corridor she told me. Then she left. You know what I felt?"

"No."

"I felt suddenly very old. I felt very old. The French

call it a *coup de vieux*. I look very old today. I should be comforting you, I suppose. But you don't deserve it really, do you? You and Anna match each other well. You cause agony in others' lives. She's always had that talent. Clearly you've just discovered it. Your wife deserves sympathy, endless, endless sympathy. But from what I have seen of her, she won't take well to sympathy. I think she won't like pity."

There was a silence. She spoke again.

"Am I different from how you remembered me?"

"Yes—very."

"All that silliness, did you think it real? It's helped me through the years. Wilbur always saw through it. Why I married him, really."

"How is Wilbur?"

"He will recover."

"Don't tell him."

"He knows."

"Anna?"

"No, not Anna. Me. He can read tragedy in my face. He said, 'I warned him. I warned him.' Did he do that?"

"Yes. Yes, he did."

"You should have listened to Wilbur. He knows everything. I'd like to attend the funeral. Will you let me know when and where?"

"Are you sure?"

"I'm very, very sure. Your son was important to me. In my own way I tried to warn him that night. But I was too subtle. Anna knew, of course. She knew what I was trying to do with my talk of Peter, and of Aston."

"She's gone to Peter, you know."

"Yes, I know. She always does. She thinks I don't

know what happened the night Aston died. My God, she thinks I don't understand why Aston died. I always pretended. Trying to keep a connection to her, I suppose. Useless. Everything I ever did was useless. I wish she'd had another mother. I suppose she does too. Ah, I'm tired. Goodbye . . . Goodbye."

I wanted to ask if Anna had told her father. But the conversation was over. I rang him immediately. I didn't want to think of what Elizabeth had said about her daughter, not now. I knew that looming ahead of me were years of emptiness. I would fill them with every word spoken about Anna, from the day I first heard of her existence.

"Charles?"

"It's kind of you to ring. I've written to you . . . and to your wife. Separately. I don't wish to talk to you. My wife and I are returning immediately to Devon. There's really nothing useful I can say, or do. I have a little knowledge of what you're going through, though of course your situation is much more terrible. That's why I know everything is useless. Everything." He sighed, and he almost whispered, "And everybody." Then the phone went dead.

I had two other calls to make, calls of honour. I rang my political agent. Into his early morning life I poured my sad tale. So few words are needed to tell a terrible story. "My son is dead."

"Oh, my God! What happened?"

"There has been a most terrible accident. It will have a difficult and shocking aftermath, John. I must tell you with profound sadness that I am resigning. We've known each other for a very long time, John. You know me well enough to accept without question that this is an irreversible decision."

"What in God's name has happened? You can't possibly ring me up at this hour with no explanation." He almost sobbed. "Oh my dear man, dear man. What can I do to help?"

"You can be the friend to me that I most need now. Accept what I am telling you. It will be clearer in the next day or so. But please respect my wishes. My career is over. You will shortly receive calls from the press and you can make a statement to the effect that I have resigned. John, I'm really sorry. I'm really very sorry." I put the phone down.

I rang my Minister at home. In a short conversation I brought my future to an end. I told him no more than I had told John. He was a man whose career was his life. He believed the same of me. He knew therefore that only a catastrophe would have led me to such a decision. Having expressed his sympathy, he said he would inform the Prime Minister on receipt of my letter of resignation.

"I will prepare it immediately. You shall have it within the hour."

I had now one final call to make. "Andrew . . ."

"I was waiting for you to call. There's been an item in the news. I'm desperately sorry. It's an appalling tragedy. What can I do to help you?"

"I want to make a statement. Urgently. To the press. You will need to clear it with the police. Can I discuss it with you?"

"Of course. The news item was very short. There were unanswered questions. What exactly happened?" His solicitor's tone was inquisitional.

"I'm not on trial, Andrew. I have already resigned, not only from the Department but also from Parliament. I want, as a private citizen, to protect my son's memory. I want to protect my wife and daughter from the kind of speculation and innuendo which will do them further damage."

"You are, and always have been, the coolest man I know. Very well. Let's work at this statement of yours. Do you want me to come round?"

"No. It's very short."

"You've already prepared it?"

"No, not fully. Anyway, there are legal aspects of which I'm not certain."

"Let's agree the basis of it. Then I can make some calls."

Eventually we agreed that Andrew would, after legal enquiries, make the following statement on my behalf:

'My son, Martyn, died last night in a tragic accident. Naturally a post mortem will be carried out. Some of the events surrounding this tragedy are sadly controversial. I have therefore resigned from my Department, and from Parliament. My resignation takes immediate effect. As a private citizen, which I will remain for the rest of my life, I would ask for privacy for my wife and for myself so that we can mourn the terrible loss of our son. And for our daughter, who has lost her most beloved brother. We will make no further comment, either now or at any time in the future.'

"I'll do it. There will be lots of questions. They won't let it slip away like this."

"No. But if it's clear that we will make no further comment they might leave us alone. My resignation removes me from every public role."

"I doubt if it will be that easy. You should prepare yourself for some very unpleasant stuff in the tabloids."

"I never read them."

"Well then, that's OK."

"Andrew, I'm holding on, just. I'm trying to save what I can for Ingrid and for Sally."

"I'm sorry. I'm sorry. It is possible to resent your control. What about Anna?"

"She's in Paris."

"Uncontactable?"

"I think so."

"The wedding aspect . . . they'll make a lot of that."

"Yes. I'm sure they will."

"Do you want me to talk to the people in the block of flats—try to silence them?"

"No. Those who are going to talk will do so. The post mortem will require them to give evidence, so it's pointless."

"That won't be held for at least three months, maybe longer."

"The cause of death is very clear. Martyn died instantly as a result of breaking his neck in the fall. I believe we can hold a private funeral in the next couple of days. Andrew, nothing in life prepared me for this conversation. It is as incredible to me as it no doubt is to you. I am trying to stay in the world of arrangements and information and planning, because I must get Ingrid and Sally onto safe ground. Then, I can perhaps go mad. That is the right, the fitting response. But not now, Andrew, not now. I need your cold professional guidance. Please."

"You'll get it. Rely on it."

"Thank you, thank you. Now I must go. I'm going to send Ingrid and Sally to Hartley with Edward. He said he would try to make arrangements for Martyn to be buried in the cemetery there."

"And you?"

"Edward has said I can use his London flat. From there I'll contact everyone who needs to keep in touch with me."

"How is Ingrid?"

"What can I say to that?"

"Nothing."

"Safe ground, Andrew. I'm trying to help them reach safe ground."

"And you?"

"Oh, me. My life is finished. But that's irrelevant now. Andrew, I'm grateful. I'll let you get on with it then."

"Yes. Goodbye."

"Goodbye, Andrew."

Though it may arrive with shocking suddenness, horror devours its prey slowly. Through hours of days and years, it spreads its sullen darkness into every corner of the being it has conquered. As hope drains like blood from a fatal wound, a heavy weakness descends. The victim slips into the underworld where he must search for new paths in what he now knows will be a permanent darkness. Horror claimed me. Ingrid and Sally would suffer terrible grief and pain. But I must keep horror from them. Then perhaps they would have a chance.

"Sally and Ingrid would like to go to the hospital before we go to Hartley." Edward had come into the study.

"I'll take them, Edward."

"Without you. I'm afraid Ingrid wants to go without you."

"I see. Edward, it's very hard. I'm worried about them."

"A little late I think, don't you?"

"Nothing you can say has any effect, Edward. I'm beyond pain at the moment. I can help Ingrid through this ordeal."

"You will make it worse by being there."

"Have you asked her, Edward?"

"No. But I am sure."

I went to the sitting room.

"Ingrid, I'm going to take you and Sally and Edward to the hospital mortuary."

Ingrid was sitting straight and tall in her chair. Her feet looked awkward, as though they were planted in the carpet. Her back was hard against the chair back. It was a body without slack, as if it knew that the slightest weakening of muscle or line would lead to total disintegration. Her face, from which the swelling had drained, was again delicate and pale, and held itself awkwardly on her neck.

Holding together a body, preserving a face, first steps on the road to survival. Grief trapped within the steel cage of the outer being is still grief trapped. Tearing at muscle and bone in a frenzy, and unable to escape, it inflicts its slow-acting wounds. Internal injuries taken to the grave, which no post mortem can reveal. Slowly, grief tires and sleeps, but never dies. In time, it grows used to its prison, and a relationship of respect develops between prisoner and jailer. I know that now, only now. Ingrid had borne me Martyn. And last night I had embraced his death and had borne it away from her. I would treasure it. And she was free of rage, and anger, and the guilt of the guiltless. Ingrid's battle now was with grief. And though grief would finally win, she would have a life. That is no mean achievement.

"I think it's better if I take you." Edward spoke.

"You too must come, Father. But I wish to go to see Martyn with his father."

Edward sighed and turned away, weeping. He was an old man defeated at the end of his life. No chance for Edward. The wound was mortal. He would not survive. I remembered an old Chinese proverb: 'Call no man happy until he is dead.' Edward's long stretch of time with only one wound—the death of his wife—had ended with this last brutality, and I saw life die in his eyes. The rest would follow.

London is no place for death. We drove through streets noisy with cars on their way to offices, cars on their way to school, buses unloading ribbons of people down grey corridors of buildings, past the violent colours of places to clothe the body, and places to feed the body. No fit route to a mortuary. There, all that remains of a life you have loved is a body you must bury.

Small emblems of respect remained from my old world. We were met discreetly. We were guided silently to what was to be our last vision of Martyn. Awe and silence are necessary in the face of death. For the tears and cries are not real—they are only echoes of a sorrow that began with the first death. And will cease with a sigh at the last.

We stood quietly, this woman and I, looking at the frozen beauty of our son. Noting how death almost became him. His pallor and his black hair, his chiselled features, were now like the marble head of a young god.

I do not know how long we stood there. Finally, Ingrid moved. Slowly, with dry eyes and lips, she kissed her son. She looked at me, and with her eyes gave me permission. But I would not. The Judas kiss is for the living. I would not defile my son further.

We did not go home again. Bags had been packed by Jonathan. Drivers had been contacted, and with the soft protective cloak of wealth wrapped around them, Ingrid, Sally, Jonathan, and Edward sped to Hartley, and to the gentle blessing of the country. To a new life. Life after Martyn. The first lap of their journey had begun.

THIRTY-FIVE

I went to Edward's flat. Later my Minister visited me there. A private letter from the Prime Minister was handed to me. Decent kindnesses, humanitarian acts of distant sympathy. There was the slow realisation by discreet visitors from my lost world that the man before them, their old protégé or rival or colleague, was falling faster and faster away from them; falling through layers of power and success, through the membranes of decency and ordinariness into a labyrinth of horror. And in its paths lurked depravity, brutality, death. And most frightening of all—chaos.

But decent men will try to do the decent thing. And they were decent men. They tried to tell me what a loss I would be. One of them even spoke with desperate sincerity the decent lie, "You can survive this. Rescind your resignation. You acted too hastily." Then his voice, full of pain, trailed off into truth.

Andrew rang. "The papers will follow their normal pattern. Your house has about ten journalists and photographers outside it. They will soon go to Hartley and also possibly find out where you are now."

"Should I tell Edward to lock the gates at Hartley?"

"Absolutely."

"So what can I expect?"

"The usual. The quality papers will concentrate on your career and your resignation. Martyn's paper will home in on the tragedy happening just before the wedding. Quite a lot of innuendo. Didn't they find you naked? The others will have a field day. They'll stop short of calling you a murderer. But you and Anna will be front-page news. There's some implication of . . . how can I put this . . . sexual games, I don't know. Oh God! Anyway, I'm warning you. This side of libel, they'll crucify you."

"How long will it last?"

"Well, you've resigned. Anna's disappeared. After the funeral it will die down. Of course, there will be further press coverage at the inquest."

"Yes, probably."

"The other angle which one bitch brought up was your marriage. Were you and Ingrid still together? Would you be getting a divorce? Investigative reporting for the good of society, you know the kind of thing."

"So it will last a week to ten days?"

"Yes, about that."

"And then, for the rest of my life! Andrew, there are many issues I will need to talk to you about, but after the funeral."

"Is there anything I can do between now and then?"

"No. I'm grateful to you for all you've done already. I'm afraid I must go now. I still have a lot of things to arrange."

To strangers I spoke of the burial of my son at Hartley. With Edward's help, times and dates were set when his body would be forever lost to us. Then I spoke again to Anna's mother. She had decided it was best not to attend the funeral. We said our goodbyes.

Edward arranged for someone to let me in via the farm. Late that night I set off for Hartley. Images of death and horror lurked behind the ghostly shadows of the trees on the road. The pain of Martyn's loss was equalled only by the pain of longing for her. The name that my voice cried out was Anna, Anna, Anna. But the tears that I shed were for him.

THIRTY-SIX

We quietly occupied the small corners of the next day that still seemed normal. Eating and drinking, bathing, walking. We gave these activities more time and attention than usual, almost ritualising them. We found it possible to make preparations for the church service and funeral in short intense bursts of phone calls and meetings. Edward had two private lines and the main phone was off the hook.

Tired, bored men with cameras, and young colourful women were glimpsed at the end of the drive. The press. I felt no animosity. My son, after all, had been one of them. Anna too had no doubt stood outside homes to report on the stricken faces of mourners. So that between the Kellogg's and the toast, eternity might clamour across the minds of her readers.

In black, shiny chariots of metal, on the following morning we drove past the weary recorders of our little story; they were frustrated by their failure yesterday to photograph or talk to anyone. The clicking and the flashing of their cameras, and the questions that the journalists mouthed through the glass, seemed as much part of the ritual of death as the chaplain, who with concerned features greeted yet another family to his house of ancient words and symbols.

Our small family, a black chorus round the grave, witnessed the impossible. The burial of Martyn. Into this scene of black, I dreamed Anna. I created her standing by the grave, dressed all in white. So white. And she threw armfuls of red roses into the open grave. The thorns, as they ripped her arms, released drops of blood into the earth and onto the white, so white, of her dress. White. White. For a second, everything was blotted out by white light. Then it was over. We sped in our black chariots back to Hartley.

Ingrid sat with me that night in Edward's study. Two people, tired unto death.

"I don't want to live with you again," she said. "Ever."

"What do you want to do?"

"I want to go away for a few months to Italy. Arthur Mandelson has offered me his place outside Rome. I'm asking Sally to come with me for a month. Jonathan can fly out to see her. Then I think she'd like to live in London with him."

"I understand. They are clearly right for each other. And after that?"

"I'll live in Hartley, I think. Maybe I will get a small place in London as well. I'll ask Paul Panten to contact Andrew and arrange whatever is necessary."

"I'll tell Andrew."

"One other thing."

"Yes."

"After tomorrow, I never want to see you again in my life. It would help me greatly to be certain of that. It will mean sacrifices. Sally's wedding . . . other family occasions . . . like funerals." She laughed bitterly.

"You have my word."

"Do you understand?"

"I do."

"That night, that strange night when you said, 'Give him to me. Give him to me,' some terrible anger left me. It flew to you. I want it out of my life for ever. You must take it with you, and go away."

"Can I see Sally sometimes?"

"Of course. But ask her not to tell me."

"I will."

"I do not ask your plans. Keep them secret from me."

"I will."

"You never loved me, you know."

"No."

"Deep down I knew that. But it seemed to suit both of us at the time."

"Yes. Oh yes, it did . . . so well."

"Is this love's revenge, do you think? Its lesson? It will not be cheated."

"Perhaps."

"I'd like to find that certain kind of love too."

I remained silent.

She sighed.

"You're right. I doubt I ever will. It may be too cruel for me. I'd be too frightened. I liked you a lot. In my own way I loved you. I don't think you realised how much." She smiled sadly. "All my old life is buried here with Martyn. At Hartley I will find my own way, as long as . . ."

"I'm out of your life."

"Yes. I'm so, so tired now. It's extraordinary but I know I'll sleep. And you?"

"I'll sit here for a while, I want to talk to Sally and Edward, then I will leave."

I watched her as she walked towards the door, her body still aching from the brimming pain of grief. She turned and smiled at me. "Goodbye. I don't mean this to sound cruel, but what a pity you didn't die, in some accident or something, last year."

"My tragedy is that I don't agree. Goodbye, Ingrid."

She closed the door behind her.

After some time I too left the room. With coffee and tears and watched by the uncomprehending eyes of Edward and Sally, I cut myself out of their lives as I would a cancer from their bodies. With a silver thread of words I tried to sew up the wounds.

I left for London. In Edward's flat I laid down my plans for the rest of my life.

THIRTY-SEVEN

"I have post from Hampstead."

It was Andrew on the phone.

"Do you want me to send it to you at Edward's flat?"

"Andrew, I want to have a talk with you—about the future. Can you come to the flat?"

"I'll come this afternoon, about four."

"OK."

He handed me a large brown packet filled with letters.

"All for me?"

"No. Quite a few for Ingrid, some for Sally."

"Can you send them to Hartley?"

"There might be some . . . well . . . crank letters."

"Can you tell?"

"Let's look at each envelope carefully."

We picked out a few that looked strange. But there was nothing sinister. It was just normal post, special cleaning service offers, sale announcements, et cetera. "The rest look safe," I said. "Send them on to Hartley."

"You won't be seeing Ingrid . . . in the next few days?" He looked at me, then glanced away.

"Andrew. Ingrid and I will not be together again, ever. I want you to liaise with Paul Panten and come to an arrangement. We're both wealthy. Ingrid must have everything that belongs to our old life. Hampstead, the paintings, everything. If you would liaise with Johnson at Albrights for a statement of affairs, we can agree on a financial settlement. Sally, of course, has her trust fund."

"And Martyn's . . . now. I'm sorry, but this is a financial conversation."

"No. Please, you are right. Yes, and Martyn's now. It automatically transferred to her if Martyn died without a family. Andrew, I need a few days to think about my own future. Can we talk on Friday?"

"By all means." He looked down at the letters. We both saw the one from France.

"I'll go now. We'll talk on Friday. I'll put everything into operation."

"Andrew, I'm profoundly grateful. No arguments from you? No advice?"

"I know you too well to try to advise you. Or perhaps too little. Till Friday." He left. I opened the letter from France. It was from Peter:

'I have a letter for you from Anna. She insisted that I should give it to you personally. Can you call me? We can discuss how and when I can do this.' There was nothing else. I rang immediately.

"Where is Anna?"

"I don't know."

"I don't believe that."

He sighed. "Please understand that what you believe or don't believe is completely irrelevant to me."

"I'm sorry. When did she leave?"

"On the day of Martyn's funeral."

"How did she know the date?"

"My God! It's hardly been a secret in the English newspapers."

"Where did she go?" He remained silent.

"I'm not asking you where she is now, just where did she go that day."

"She went, my friend, to visit the grave of her brother."

For a moment I was blinded by the white light of shock.

"Alone?"

"All alone. I will say it once again. The last I saw of Anna was the day of Martyn's funeral. She left my home in a taxi. She said goodbye to me. I think this time she meant it."

"What did she wear?"

"What? A white dress. She said she was going to buy roses for his grave. Then she was gone."

"Red, I suppose?" As if in a dream.

"I don't know what colour. This is a hopeless conversation. Now, as my last act for Anna, do I bring the letter to you, or do you come to collect it?"

"I will come to collect it."

"You'd better come to my apartment then."

I took the address.

"Tomorrow at six."

"Tomorrow at six."

THIRTY-EIGHT

The apartment had all the understated elegance and deceptive simplicity I had come to associate with Peter Calderon. He was a very clever man. The kind of man clever enough to hide his brilliance. The kind of man who would quickly learn from the few mistakes he would make. Like the kind of mistakes he'd made with Anna, long ago.

"This is very kind." I started conversationally.

"No. It is not kind. It is a duty."

"Ah!"

"Here is the letter. I'd rather you did not read it here."

"Why? Do you know what's in it?"

"No."

"But you could hazard a guess?"

"No. I could give you my professional opinion. But then you probably wouldn't listen."

"I'm listening now."

"Anna will not find it possible to continue her relationship with you."

"Why not? Oh, I know the obvious reasons."

"You mean guilt? No, no, Anna could handle the guilt all right. Actually most people can. For example, you managed perfectly well to deceive your son. One barely finds it necessary to refer to the minor betrayal of your wife. Yet you are here days after your son has died, his death undoubtedly all but occasioned by you. You are here to search for Anna. So please! Guilt, guilt, its pious expression alone is in fact today's great absolution. Just say the guilt prayer, 'I feel guilty,' and hey presto, that's the punishment. The guilt is the punishment. So punished, and therefore cleansed, one can continue with the crime."

"Why then? Why can't she continue with me?"

"Because it's only now that she has finally said good-bye to Aston. Anna has spoken to me of your relationship with her. You were part of the healing process. You were a vital part. The outer limits which you visited were—how can I put it?—a journey which you and she were destined to make. But one which is over. It is over." He looked at me. "At least at this moment in time it is over for Anna."

"The last thing she said to me was, it's over. But I won't accept it."

"Because it's not yet over for you."

"It never will be."

"Maybe not. Maybe not. But you will only be a visitor now to old views, old rooms, old dreams. Perhaps that's enough for you."

"I won't give up."

"Read the letter. Then decide. Be grateful you made the journey at all. Few people do. Perhaps it's just as well. Tragedy almost always follows. But then, if you'd known a year ago?"

I looked at him.

"My wife wished I'd died. Not lived to do this."

"But then you'd never have lived at all. Would you?"

"No."

He smiled, as he led me to the door. "Few regret the experience."

"Do you?"

"I never had that kind of experience with Anna. Neither did Martyn. In that one way you were truly made for each other. Men and women find all sorts of ways to be together, all sorts of ways. Yours was high and dangerous. Most of us stay on the lower paths."

THIRTY-NINE

In a green grove in the Tuileries Gardens I found a quiet place, leaning against a plane tree, to read my fate:

I must take myself back from you. I was a fatal gift. I was the gift of pain which you sought so eagerly, pleasure's greatest reward. Though bound together in a savage minuet, whoever and whatever we truly are or were meant to be, soared free. Like aliens on Earth we found in each and every step the language of our own lost planet. You needed pain. It was mine you hungered for. But though you do not believe it, your hunger is fully satisfied. Remember you have your own pain now. It will be 'everything, always.' Even if you found me, I would not be there. Don't search for something you already have. The hours and days allotted to us and now for ever gone are also 'Everything. Always.'

Anna

A leaf fell slowly to earth like a giant green tear. I had no tears to shed. I felt my body, touching my arms and chest. This thing will need to be housed somewhere until it is finally ready for burial. I must keep my promise to Ingrid—live, live on. But I needed a coffin, of sorts.

I stood up to walk away. A child in frantic pursuit of a ball crashed into me. We looked at each other, and some wisdom made her race away from me, crying.

FORTY

It takes a remarkably short time to withdraw from the world. Certain basic affairs, of course, must be formalised. Andrew deals with all bills, and transfers a monthly figure for living expenses. Personal letters forwarded from Hampstead or Hartley are destroyed by him. The supply dries up with considerable speed. Few people have my address—Sally, of course, Peter Calderon, just in case. But I know, deep down, there is no reprieve.

I had only one formal public appearance to make, the inquest. The verdict was accidental death. Ingrid, Sally, and Edward did not attend. Of course much was made of the non-attendance of Anna Barton.

I have an apartment in a small street in the city in which I now live. I chose it carefully. Its white walls and white wood-panelled ceilings guided my choice. Since then I have added white blinds to its high windows, a white carpet, white bookcases. In time I also bought embossed white paper to hide the covers of the books. I found the shades, however subtle, too much.

The cleaning lady who comes each day for two hours dislikes the fact that I sit and watch her. But I have to. Once she brought red roses. She couldn't get the white lilies I had ordered. Agonies began, which took me days to bank down.

I have two large pictures, which are turned to the wall when she comes. I know she would try to turn them round if I weren't there. They hang opposite each other, in the small hallway that leads from the main living room to the bathroom. Though the photographer had difficulty enlarging them to the size I wanted, he managed eventually. Mounted on a white background they stand about five feet high. Or lie.

I have a routine. I exercise. I bought a book based on my father's old regime—thirteen minutes of naval exercises each morning. Then breakfast. Reading. Always the classics. There's a lifetime's reading there. I certainly haven't got a lifetime left. While the flat is being cleaned I listen to language tapes. I take one holiday each year in the sun, always to a different country. I challenge myself to have at least a grasp of the language of the country I shall visit. This is my third year of such challenge.

After my cleaning lady leaves I take a long walk. I have a light lunch at a café. Then I return to my white haven and continue my reading or I listen to music. Just as often I sit for hours letting the white purity of my room invade me.

I hear from Sally regularly. Wilbur died. Not, after all, from a heart attack, but in an automobile accident. It was Edward who died from heart failure, within a year of Martyn's death. I thought . . . I feared that might happen.

Ingrid has remarried, a captain of industry, who has just received a knighthood. Sally hasn't married yet. She and Jonathan are still together. 'It's not,' she wrote to me some time ago, 'that I don't trust love. It's that I no longer know what it is.'

I am never lonely. My favourite place in the world, my world, is the long narrow corridor to the bathroom. There I sit sometimes in the evening, gazing at the life-size photograph of Martyn. I change the position of the chair, so the perspective changes all the time.

Once I simply stood in front of his image with my arms touching the sides of the frame. For hours and hours I tried to search for the knowledge in his eyes that his life would not be as he had hoped. But caught for ever by the camera in a moment of laughter, power, and beauty, his face seems to burst from its trap of technology and glass with triumphant, defiant life.

Sometimes I gaze at Anna . . . at a photograph taken during her engagement weekend at Hartley. I took it from the study as I left Hartley for the last time. Quizzically, she gazes back at me. The movement of her dark feathered hair in the breeze is at odds with the steady, unsmiling eyes and solemn face. I remember how rarely she laughed. When I search her face from all perspectives I can find in it only a passive power, that seems to say 'I am not caught, for I do not move.'

Her years of silence are presaged in that face.

Desire rarely troubles me. Once (and since then I have ceased to drink) I laid her picture on the floor. Stretching out on it, in what I thought was a rage of grief, I found myself instead lost in a storm of the body's desperation. As I cried out in agony there came semen and tears.

And I remembered what she had written of the night Aston had come to her bed: 'Semen and tears are the symbols of the night.'

FORTY-ONE

I wear casual clothes now, and often dark glasses. I find all colour offends me.

I pack very little for my short holiday. Germany this year.

The airport is hideous, crowded, colourful, and noisy. I turn a corner. All becomes quiet. It seems to me that other people are in sudden slow motion.

Anna appears before me. She moves towards me. She takes my dark glasses from me. She looks into and beyond me as though gathering herself from me for ever. Silently, she wrestles for the part of her I still keep. She is all powerful. It is an act of repossession. My body seems to fall in on itself, to become a song or a scream, a sound so high, so thin, that it shatters bone and tears muscle.

I know my heart has been ripped. It is disintegrating. I fall to my knees. It is an act of worship and defeat. My lips brush the cotton of her dress. Its summer garden colours of green and yellow are acid in my eyes. Someone rushes to help me. Anna simply walks on.

"Do you need a doctor?" The young man helps me to my feet.

"No. No, I'm fine. I am a doctor."

I rush back in the direction she has taken. I see her join a man holding a small child by the hand. He turns slightly towards her and Peter Calderon's lips brush her hair. From this perspective, I see that the slight disarray of her skirt is due to pregnancy.

I find a taxi. As it speeds back to the flat I doubt now I will ever leave, I wonder how long my body will survive. Not long, not long, I hope.

Final thoughts come to me. With a sigh I close the door.

Dying, possibly years before the idiotic mechanism of my body finally surrenders, I whisper to myself and to the silent faces in the hall, "At least I am certain of the truth now."

For those of you who doubt it—this is a love story.

It is over.

Others may be luckier.

I wish them well.

A NOTE ON THE TYPE

The text of this book was set in Bembo,
a facsimile of a type face cut by one of the most
celebrated goldsmiths of his time, Francesco Griffo,
for Aldus Manutius, the Venetian printer, in 1495.
The face was named for Pietro Bembo, the author
of the small treatise entitled *De Aetna* in which it first
appeared. Through the research of Stanley Morison,
it is now acknowledged that all old-face type
designs up to the time of William Caslon
can be traced to the Bembo cut.
The present-day version of Bembo was intro-
duced by The Monotype Corporation, London,
in 1929. Sturdy, well balanced, and finely
proportioned, Bembo is a face of rare
beauty and great legibility
in all of its sizes.

Composed by Brevis Press,
Bethany, Connecticut
Printed and bound by The Haddon Craftsmen,
Scranton, Pennsylvania
Designed by Mia Vander Els